TYREAN MARTINSON

LIFT OFF

RAYATANA, BOOK 1

Copyright © 2020 by Tyrean Martinson

LIFTOFF

The Rayatana Series, Book One

All rights reserved. Except as permitted under the U.S. Copyright Act of 1976, no part of this publication may be reproduced, distributed, or transmitted in any form or by any means, or stored in a database or retrieval system, without prior permission of the author.

This is a work of fiction. Names, characters, brands, places, and events are either a product of the author's imagination or used fictitiously. Any similarity to real persons, living or dead, is coincidental and not intended by the author.

Wings of Light Publishing
Gig Harbor, WA, USA

Cover Art and Interior Design by Carrie Butler

Professionally Edited by Chrys Fey

DEDICATION

For the first time in a long time, I wrote a book for me, for the adult I am now, the teen I once was, and even the younger child deep inside me. This book is for anyone who has ever felt stuck at a crossroads, challenged by family history, or desiring an escape on a rocket ship. I wrote it during April of 2020, to keep my mind off COVID and the world at large, and to escape into a fantastical realm of space adjacent to our reality. It is dedicated to creatives, daydreamers, romantics, hopefuls, action-sci-fi movie fans, and especially those who have a little bit of all that inside them.

01

AMAYA

Amaya didn't like matinees, but they were cheap, and money was tight since her parents' divorce and her mom's decision to move back to the small city of her childhood in Western Washington, in the shadow of Mt. Rainier. Amaya didn't like it. She missed her besties, martial arts classes, the California sun, everything about her old life. She'd lost so much. At seventeen, she should be getting ready for college, but all she wanted, as she sat in the dark movie theater, was a sense of home. All summer long, this old movie theater welcomed her in and wrapped her up in the smell of popcorn and licorice. Something about this place just felt right.

Amaya leaned back into the surprisingly comfortable red vinyl seat and put a hand on her necklace. Three intertwined ovals were raised above the surface of the front, while the back held a triangle of three stars on one side and a shooting star on the other. Her maternal grandfather had made it, and her maternal grandmother had blessed it. It linked her to them, to belonging somewhere. Her chest ached, thinking about their sudden deaths, just months before her parents' divorce.

"Popcorn?" Amaya's new friend Jessi held out the bucket, bringing Amaya back to the moment.

Amaya nodded and took a handful. She didn't eat any, but the strong, buttery smell held her thoughts at bay.

On the other side of Jessi, Natalie offered up their shared soda.

Amaya smiled, but she shook her head. Jessi and Natalie were really sweet, probably the nicest, most normal friends she'd had in her life. They talked about boys, movies, romance novels, and school. And they were open about race and ethnicity, which Amaya appreciated. She'd heard racist remarks her whole life because of her burnt sienna skin, but Jessi and Natalie accepted her. They didn't even care that she didn't know what her ethnicity was exactly. Despite her many questions, her parents didn't want her to know about her roots. It made no sense and drove her crazy. All her mom cared about was signing Amaya up for martial arts, survival skills, archery, and gymnastics. Amaya's old friends and private schools had also been vetted by her mom. Despite her mom's reasoning for her paranoia, something always felt off, like her mom was just one step beyond the normal helicopter moms.

Jessi nudged her with the popcorn bucket again. At some point in her melancholy, Amaya had eaten her popcorn. She took another handful, inhaled the scent, and then forced her gaze up to the screen.

In the movie, a teen girl and a teen guy stood awkwardly at a bus stop. He was offering to take her out for coffee or ice cream or anything. Amaya wanted to fall into the silly romantic vibe of it, but she was struggling to let go of everything today. She glanced over at her friends, who were staring up at the screen in anticipation. Jessi and Natalie loved romance with the fervor of the uninitiated. They were so much fun that it had been easy to be drawn into light conversation and boy gossip with them, even reading romances and watching cheesy movies.

They had the whole theater to themselves, and the air conditioning had been set to freezing. Shivering in summer shorts with a thin, long-sleeve top, Amaya curled her legs to her chest and tried, again, to lose herself in the movie. She hadn't seen it before, but she had checked out the book from the library.

The film jerked to a sudden stop right as the guy reached for the girl's hand.

Amaya sighed.

"Hey, we didn't even get to the first awkward kiss," Jessi groaned.

Then all the little lights along the aisles winked out, the comforting neon of the exit sign disappeared, and the movie screen went dark. The theater rumbled.

"Earthquake!" Amaya shouted, grabbing for her friends as she struggled to stand. The ground rolled, and she fell forward onto the next row of seats.

Jessi and Natalie screamed.

Amaya fought to right herself and settled for rolling sideways off the seats.

The earth had stopped moving, but Jessi kept screaming, and Natalie sounded as though she was crying.

"It's okay," Amaya said. "It stopped. Jessi, take deep breaths. We're going to be okay."

"Okay," Jessi said in a ragged voice.

A beam of light pierced the darkness, followed by a calm, deep voice. "Everyone all right in here?"

"I think so," Amaya said. "Can you lead us out?"

The flashlight beam swept over Jessi and Natalie and landed on Amaya. She self-consciously tugged at the frayed hem of her shirt. Then she reached out to Jessi. "C'mon, we're getting out of here."

"Okay," Jessi whispered. She took Amaya's hand and rose to her feet.

Natalie stood behind her and took Jessi's other hand.

Amaya knew she should be prepared for anything, thanks to her mom's training, but for now, holding hands felt better. At least they could anchor each other in the darkness.

FLICKERING

A flickering red light appeared in the corner by the exit door, revealing the edges of the nearest escape. It wasn't the exit sign, though, but a separate bulb encaged in metal. Amaya had seen it before, but it had never been lit.

Is it their emergency backup system?

The flashlight beam piercing the darkness revealed Sol Anderson. Tall, with wavy midnight hair and olive skin, Sol was already the subject of many conversations among the girls. He could even make the dorky movie theater uniform look good.

He beckoned with his hand. "Let's get out of here, all right?" Instead of leading them toward the lobby, he led them toward the exit under the alarm light.

"Why this way?" Amaya asked, remembering how the back exit went out into a small, ugly parking lot overgrown with scrubby bushes and trash.

"Trust me," Sol said. His voice oozed charm.

Amaya eyed him. *How is he so calm after an earthquake?*

Suspicion had her inching closer to her friends. "I don't like this," she whispered to them.

"Don't worry. Two steps from here and you'll be through the back door and in the summer sunshine," Sol said. He stepped forward and threw open the exit door.

Sunlight blazed into the theater.

Jessi let go of Amaya's hand and bolted out the door, with Natalie right behind her.

Amaya didn't move. She stared at Sol, noticing the rips on the front of his uniform for the first time. "What happened?"

"Don't worry about me." Sol took his hand off the door to reach out for her. At that moment, the theater lurched to the side.

As the world spun and dipped around her, Amaya stumbled sideways into Sol's solid chest and clutched his arm. She trembled when the air rippled. "What's happening?"

"I'm sorry." He wrapped his other arm around her waist and held her close as the ground rocked beneath them again.

"What?" Amaya pushed at his arm. "Let go of

me!"

"I can't do that. It's not safe." He pulled her back a step, gently but firmly guiding her.

Amaya resisted. *I have to get to the door. I might be able to make it out.*

When the theater tilted, and the old, scrubby lot fell away, Amaya fought back a scream. *The movie theater is rising.*

In the parking lot below, Natalie and Jessi shouted and pointed up at her.

Terrified, Amaya broke free from Sol and stepped toward the opening, but Sol moved in front of her and pulled the door firmly shut, locking it in place. "We can't have that door open for liftoff."

As Amaya's glimpse of her friends and her world disappeared, she glared at Sol. *What does he mean by liftoff?*

Sol reached out for her, but she backed away. The darkness surrounding her represented a possible hiding place, so she scrambled toward the direction of the seats under the flickering alarm beacon.

Sol clicked his flashlight on again, and the beam swept over her as she crawled up the first step to the seats.

"Amaya, where do you think you're going?" He followed her easily into the seating area.

"Away from you!" She vaulted over the railing between the seats and the exit hallway that led out into the concessions area.

FORWARD

Charging forward, Amaya didn't expect Sol to catch her. She'd always been one of the fastest runners in school, but Sol caught her in seconds and wrapped his arms around her just as she reached the doorway.

She fought against him, and he held her tight. Fear coursed through her, and she lashed out with her feet, connecting with his ankle, his knee.

"Amaya, please, if I let you go, will you give me a chance to explain?"

"Let me go now!"

"I don't want you to get hurt."

"Prove it!"

He let her go, just as she threw an uppercut into his jaw.

He blinked, and tears sprang into his eyes, but he stepped back, holding his hands in front of his face.

Amaya edged away from him.

Sol angled his body and held out his arms. "Amaya, please, let me tell you a few things before we strap in for liftoff. I don't think you're ready."

"Ready for what?"

He put his hand to his jaw. "Well, maybe we aren't ready for you, actually." He winced as he touched the spot where she'd landed her punch. "You know how my aunt and uncle opened the theater and I moved here to help them run the place?"

"I didn't move here that long ago myself, but I heard something about that." Maybe if she kept him talking about himself, he would stop paying attention to her every move. Then she could run again.

"Well, that's not exactly the truth." He paused and glanced up at the ceiling, as if figuring out what to say.

She edged toward the door. *I have to keep him distracted.*

He stepped toward her again. "We're from another part of the galaxy."

She stopped moving. *Is he nuts?*

"But this theater can't be a…spaceship." Normally, she'd never believe in spaceships, but she had seen the theater leave the ground. It was the one partially-lunatic but reasonable explanation she had. She put her fingers around her necklace to rub the intertwined ovals embedded in layers of metal. It usually comforted her. Not this time.

She looked at Sol. Although the flashlight swung on a strap on his wrist, it gave off a circle of light that surrounded them. The alarm flickered over them in bursts, revealing that Sol's eyes were dark green, not blue. Unless they had changed.

She glared at him. "Why?"

He frowned. "Why what?"

The bruise on his chin was turning mottled red. Guilt filled her. *Did he have bruises in other places?* In her panic she had been kicking pretty hard. An apology was on the tip of her tongue, but she shook her head. *What am I thinking? Apologize to an alien who had kidnapped me in his movie theater-spaceship?*

04

DON'T PRETEND

"Don't pretend you don't know what I'm talking about! Why did you keep me from jumping? Are you the aliens that experiment on people?" Goosebumps rose on her arms. She wanted to run somewhere, anywhere, away. *If I can get my phone out without him noticing, I can call for help. I think my dad might take my call for this.*

"What? No. We aren't like that," Sol said. "It just happened."

"It just happened?" She stepped toward him again, raising her fist. All the bad events of the last year swept through her memory. This was one more terrible event in a list of terrible events. Her life was shattered, and he had the gall to tell her he'd accidentally held her back from trying to find her normal again? The ball of anger inside her rose to rest behind her eyes. Her mom had always told her not to look on people in anger, but her mom wasn't here. Amaya glared at Sol. "I'm stuck on some stupid, ridiculous movie theater-spaceship, and 'it just happened'?"

She shook her fist, and he stepped back out of her reach, colliding with the wall on the other side of the hallway. "You held onto me when the ship lifted off. I could have jumped, but you kept me here. Don't tell me, 'it just happened'!" She put her fist against his chest and leaned against his breastbone.

"Amaya, your eyes…they're…you're…"

She lowered her gaze and stepped back. No one liked her eyes when she was angry. Waves of anger and shame coursed through her. All the times she'd been told to keep her gaze down; she was tired of it, so she glared at him again. "How did your uniform get ripped? You didn't tell me."

He held a hand in front of his eyes, as if he was afraid to look at her. "Amaya, please forgive me," he said, "but we have to get strapped in. Really, I'll explain everything once we're safe."

She stiffened her shoulders. "You will tell me what happened to your uniform and what is happening to this ship, and you will let me go home."

After a long moment, he said, "I promise to take you home as soon as we can. You have my Word, my Bond." He held out his hand.

When Amaya put her fingers over his, a jolt ran through her. She jerked away from him, stepping back. *Where had that come from?*

His eyes crinkled, and his lips quirked into a semi-smirk.

"Don't," she snapped.

"Don't what?"

"I'm not interested in alien cooties." As soon as the words came out of her mouth, she regretted them. She sounded as if she was nine years old or something. She glanced toward the door again.

"Cooties? I don't think I'm familiar with that term." Sol tilted his head lower and stepped toward her. "You'll have to explain it to me sometime."

"Aren't we in a hurry?"

He pointed to the exit. "I promise the seats are far more comfortable in the command booth." He held out his hand.

Amaya ignored it. "The concession stand holds alien technology as well as tasty popcorn?"

"The command booth isn't the concession stand. It's the box office," he said.

Amaya nodded and stalked toward the front of the theater, determined not to show any more fear.

HER TERMS

Entering the lobby on her own terms, Amaya felt stronger, better, in charge of the situation. The lobby looked mostly the same, with the bright red carpeting, the posters for upcoming movies on one side, and the posters for previous movies on the other. She inhaled the scents of buttered popcorn and licorice mixed with something else—rocket fuel? Her anxiety increased, and she put her hand over her necklace again. This theater had felt so normal, so home-like, filled with old stories and wonder, but now it was something else.

The concession stand looked relatively normal, but the box office and the theater entrance had transformed. The seats behind the box office counter were still there, but the counter held an array of lights and gadgets. The front doors and the floor-to-ceiling windows were now covered with a strange metal and a screen overlay.

How it was possible, Amaya didn't know and she really didn't want to know, as long as she could find a way back home.

In the box office, now a command center, Sol's aunt and uncle looked down at separate consoles. The front screen showed sky, fields, and approaching objects on the horizon.

Amaya stopped in her tracks and stared at the screen. "What are those?"

"Oh no." Sol groaned. "Come on." He grabbed her hand and attempted to pull her into the command center.

"No way." She planted her feet.

"Do you want to stay safe or get thrown around the room when we get hit?"

"Hit?" She let him pull her toward his aunt and uncle, who looked up with shocked expressions on their faces.

FREAKING OUT

Freaking out, but trying not to show it, Amaya gave Sol's aunt and uncle a nod as he rushed her toward one of the consoles in the box office. It had an interesting chair, like a barber shop chair with a five-point harness.

When Sol reached around her to strap her in, she stopped him. "I know how to strap into a seat like this."

He let go of the straps, but something slammed into the movie-theater spaceship and he ended up in her lap, clutching one of the straps above her shoulder.

"Sorry." He pushed himself away, and then he strapped into a chair near her.

"Sol, you have some explaining to do," Sol's uncle stated as he typed at his control deck.

Sol nodded. "Yes, sir."

His aunt made a chopping motion with her hand. "There's no time for this. Punch it, Geral!"

Geral punched a button on his console, and the ship's engines whined.

Amaya gripped her seat belts hard. *I never trained for this!*

A steering-stick, with a half-circular wheel, rose out of the floor by Geral's chair. "Exiting Earth's atmosphere in 5, 4, 3, 2, 1." He pulled the stick toward him.

The engines screamed, and the movie-theater spaceship shot forward.

The g-forces slammed Amaya into the back of her seat, and she struggled to take slow breaths as the ship rose higher and higher above the Earth.

Sol's aunt shouted over the engine noise. "Geral, defensive maneuvers. Sol, as soon as we clear the atmosphere, aim for their engines. We don't want to give them any more reason to blow us apart."

"Got it, Prya."

"Yes, Captain," Sol said.

What does she mean by 'any more reason'? Amaya wanted to ask what other reason someone would have to blow anyone out of the sky, but she turned her gaze to the giant screens, previously the windows of the box office, and watched them streak toward the sun. Another screen showed their rear view, and smaller screens showed other views from around the ship. It felt unreal, impossible, but they were apparently being chased by three ships, all outfitted with light-based or laser-based weapons.

Amaya hadn't had Physics yet at school, and even if she had, she wasn't sure she'd be prepared to describe what she was seeing. It felt like a movie, but one in an HD, 3D, surround sound, and full movement theater. *How is it possible I'm surviving space travel? Aren't astronauts specially trained for this? What about gravity? How am I feeling gravity in space? Am I being pranked?*

Several laser beams streaked toward the ship.

Amaya's grip on her shoulder straps became white-knuckled as she sent up a quick prayer and braced for impact.

GRAVITY

"Gravity disengaged for maneuvering," Geral warned. "The inertial dampeners on this ship are old. Prepare yourselves."

The lights in the command booth changed from flashing red to bright green, making Amaya feel as though she really was in a spaceship, except when she glanced over her shoulder to see the popcorn and snacks floating around in the enclosed snack booth. She'd wondered why the booth was encased in plexiglass, and now she knew. But she didn't have more than a few seconds to think about it when Geral twisted the joystick in front of him and jabbed the controls with his other hand.

Gravity disappeared at the same time the ship dipped, swerved, and rotated. Most of the laser weapons streaked past them, but one hit the ship with an impact that shook them in their seats.

Bile rose to Amaya's throat, and she clamped

her mouth shut, trying to swallow. She was determined not to puke in the middle of spaceship battle.

"Put your right palm on the armrest and push the orange cross button," Sol said.

She glanced at him and then at the armrest. A tiny button flashed.

"It will help with gravity sickness."

Amaya didn't want anti-vomit medication meant for aliens, but when Geral pulled another fancy maneuver, which sent the ship rotating and diving, she slammed her hand on the armrest and touched the button. A tiny light lit up her wrist, and the strange sensation of something warm flowed into her vein.

"It's a photo-medicine."

She nodded, not trusting herself to speak. The nausea was subsiding, and she swallowed back the bile in her throat. *Nasty.* She would definitely need to brush her teeth. Did aliens brush their teeth? She glanced at Sol. He was picture perfect. *Ugh.*

Sol was staring at his console screen, a holographic display that hovered in front of his seat. Amaya wondered if she had one of those. She studied the armrest display. The orange button wasn't flashing anymore. *Is my seat reading my biological signs?* She didn't know.

The chair contained three other buttons: blue

with stars on it, green with five parallel lines, and yellow with a triangle. *What do any of them mean?* She didn't know if she should touch anything, though. The others knew what they were doing. Or so she hoped.

Glancing over at Sol, she noticed he had a target screen in the middle of his holo-display. He aimed for an attacking ship and hit a button. One of their weapons streaked toward the ship, which attempted evasion. Instead of getting out of the way, though, the ship flew into the weapon fire, and the weapon hit it dead center. The whole thing split apart.

"Sol!" Prya shouted.

"I tried to hit their engines. They flew into my fire!"

"I saw the whole thing. I have a clear view of his screen," Amaya said, trying to help out Sol.

"All right," Prya said, with a voice tight with resignation. "New plan. Geral, get us out of here."

Geral hit several buttons on his console, and the ship spun again. He pulled back on his stick, and they streaked toward the sun.

Amaya tensed up, fighting the g-forces pushing her into her seat.

Geral turned the ship slightly and shouted, "Brace for ZIG!"

Amaya wanted to ask what he meant, but the g-forces they had experienced during the space fight were nothing compared to the weight bearing against her now. Her vision flickered, dark spots closed in, and she closed her eyes. When she opened them again, a completely different sun and set of stars shone through the giant screens. The urge to puke returned with a vengeance, and she bent over her chair. But nothing came.

"The photo-medicine suppresses even the most extreme responses to space travel," Sol explained.

08

HOW

"How?" Amaya gasped.

"Well, I'm not actually sure how the photo-medicine works to suppress physical reactions to extreme space maneuvers, but—"

"I'm sure she meant, 'how is any of this possible,' Sol," Prya interrupted.

"How are you all so normal-looking and sounding? How do you speak English if you're aliens? Why America? Why not New Zealand or Australia or Japan or Morocco? And why are there other aliens attacking us?"

Prya's mouth twitched. Her bushy eyebrows rose. It was as if she was amused and surprised at the same time. "Good questions, all. Ones that can be answered when we are sure of our safety and we can get you to Med-bay."

Amaya could see Prya's eyes move towards her console and knew she needed to act immediately if she wanted to get the captain's attention. "Wait, I need to call my dad. He's in Earth's Space Defense Force. I think he would help me get home, and he'd want to stop any aliens from attacking Earth," Amaya heard the anger in her voice, but she couldn't seem to hold it back. *He hasn't talked to me in months, but aliens kidnapping his only child should get his attention, right?*

"The Space Defense Force is primarily an American cause, underfunded and unlikely to be of help to us, especially now that we are in a different solar system. Let's find a safe place to rest, and then we'll discuss our options." Prya stated firmly.

Geral swiveled in his seat so he faced the center of their group. Amaya noticed he had a golden glow in his eyes, one she had never noticed before. The glow faded as he spoke. "Good news. We're in the neutral zone, near a planet with a small port, nothing exciting or of political import, but it's a safe place we can stop for…decision-making." He glanced at Sol and then Amaya before resting his gaze on Prya.

Amaya squirmed in her seat. She didn't want any decisions made about her without her consent. "Please, somehow, I would like to go home."

"When that's possible, that will happen," Prya said. "Sol has dishonored you, and he is in your debt until he makes amends. A Terr always keeps his Word, or he dies trying. Am I clear, Nephew?"

"Yes, Aunt, er, Captain Prya." Sol nodded and

put his fist to his heart and unbuckled to stand up. "I am in your debt. I will make amends." He hesitated, holding his hand out and gazing intensely at Amaya. "My Word as a Terr is my Bond. My Bond and my Word are yours, Amaya of Earth."

"Okay." Amaya nodded, and then she saw the raised eyebrows on Prya's face. *Am I not being formal enough?* She put her hand in his. "I accept your Bond and your Word. I will hold you to your Bond and…keep your Word in my heart." She wasn't sure why she'd added the last part; it was something her grandparents always said to each other.

A jolt ran from his hand to hers, even stronger than the one she'd felt before. *What was that?*

Sol's eyes widened, shimmered slightly with flecks of gold, before returning to their normal jade. "Thank you, Amaya."

Heat rushed to her face, and she dipped her head, not sure why she suddenly felt such a strong swell of emotion. *Now was not the time to be developing a serious crush on an alien.*

"Wait—" Geral began, holding up one hand.

"Let it be," Prya commanded. She gave Amaya a full once-over, as if inspecting her from her curly hair to her small feet. "You, Amaya, will hold Solomon Gryas Terr to his Bond, which he has given you, in full authority as an adult of our people. You will keep his Word in your heart. That is a true vow. One I will not forget as your witness, as his aunt and his captain." She raised her chin. "May I know your full name, Amaya, who holds a Terr to his Word and his Bond?"

"Amaya…Amaya Iris Benson." Suddenly, Amaya wasn't sure what she had signed up for when she had answered Sol. *Have I made an error in protocol?* She didn't know how to ask the questions she needed, without making things worse.

"It is good to meet you, Amaya Iris Benson, Oath-holder. I am Captain Prya Terr. This is my mate, Geral Terr, Navigation Officer and Disavowed from the Terr family heritage."

"Nice to meet you," Amaya said. She wasn't sure what being an Oath-holder or being Disavowed meant to these people, but Prya sounded proud.

Geral raised his fist to his heart. "You do Earth proud, Amaya Iris Benson, Oath-holder." He swiveled his chair forward. "Shall I lay the course, Captain, my love?"

"Yes. Take us in."

Sol had taken his seat and put on his safety straps again, but he kept glancing over at Amaya with an expression she couldn't read. This day couldn't get any stranger.

As Geral maneuvered the ship, two enemy ships blinked into the space around them.

"I thought you made our ZIG untraceable?"

"I thought so, too." Geral hit the control panels, but the laser weapons came in too fast, smacking the ship on both sides.

"They've taken out the side engines. I've got planetary thrusters and the lifter."

"Shall I open fire?" Sol asked.

"No," Prya said. "Geral, get us on planet and out of sight, if possible."

Geral fiddled with his control panel, and the ship plunged full speed toward the planet.

Amaya bit back the urge to scream.

When they breached the atmosphere, the ship grew hot, and then cool again.

"Mountains. Good," Geral said as he yanked and prodded at the controls. The ship slowed and banked to skim over the top of the nearest white-capped mountain.

A loud bang reverberated throughout the ship.

"The lifter's gone!" Geral shouted.

They dropped toward another mountain. Geral turned the ship again, escaping the hard ridge of snow but dove them deeper into a valley, with trees below. The ship skidded over the tops of the trees and then crashed into them, burying the nose deep in the purple pine-needled forest. They came to a slow stop.

IMPRESSIVE

Amaya kept her eyes open during the entire crash, but she had to unclench her fingers from her harness. She did this now, one finger at a time, trying to let go of her fear with a deep breath and prayer exercise. This was interrupted by Sol's aunt.

"Impressive. Very impressive," Captain Prya said. She gazed at Amaya, put her forefinger to her head, and then to her heart. "Most planet-dwellers would have been screaming through that landing."

Amaya's cheeks burned. Not screaming had been an act of sheer will.

"Controlled crash," Geral corrected. "It was no landing." He poked at his instrument panel a few more times before unstrapping himself from his seat. "We appear to be stable, but the trees underneath us may give out at any moment. I set our camouflage. We need to work together to get the grapplers set. If the Triple One who rules The Great Galaxy and her chosen Rayatana favor us, we'll be safe long enough to get supplies and make repairs."

"Let it be so," Captain Prya said. "I know we can make it through this, Geral." She unstrapped herself from her chair. "I will help you." When she stood, Amaya remembered just how tall Prya was. She hadn't thought of it while they were in the middle of flight, but Prya stood taller than any other woman she'd ever met. Geral and Sol were shorter than her, although they all shared the same midnight hair.

"What can I do?" Amaya asked, unlatching her straps.

"Sol should take you to Med-bay, where you can gain information about our culture and he can get his injuries healed." Prya reached out and put her hand on Sol's chin. "What happened? I didn't notice anyone land a blow on you during the fight earlier."

"That was me," Amaya said. "I'm sorry. He was keeping me from leaving."

"You gave him this bruise?" Prya cocked her head to the side and gave Amaya a once-over again, as if inspecting her strength.

"I really don't like feeling trapped."

"It was my fault, Aunt. Her friends were out, but then the ship lurched with liftoff, and I didn't think she'd make the jump, so I grabbed her."

Prya glared at him. "We'll speak on this later.

Your behavior with women needs correction in many areas. Your mother informed me of this, but I waited to see it for myself. Your Bond to Amaya is the first step you've taken on a lifelong journey of redemption. I'm sure Amaya will keep you in line."

"Aunt, no matter what you've heard, I would never…I didn't mean to…" Sol sputtered as his aunt turned toward Amaya.

Amaya's stomach fluttered with nerves, and she fought the urge to move away from Prya, who towered over her.

"I applaud you for your strength of will and knowing how to defend yourself, Amaya, but would you really have jumped?"

"I don't know." Amaya said. "The theater… ship was rising fast. I thought…I thought I could have made it, but I don't know."

"Then he saved you, in his foolish way. Think on this. I will speak to you later, as well." She pivoted and followed Geral out of the control booth, leaving Amaya alone with Sol.

"Is she always like that?" Amaya asked him.

"Yes." He smiled. "I'm surprised you noticed."

"What's that supposed to mean?"

"As we say, roughly translated, those who are juiced from the same fruit understand one another."

"Um. Juiced?" Amaya raised her eyebrows at him.

"Have similar attitudes."

"Hmph." Amaya snorted. "How is the Med-bay supposed to help me understand your culture?"

"It's…well, you'll see." He shrugged, and then he led her out of the command booth.

She caught up to him and walked in step with him, over to the snack station with its weird, plexiglass windows. "So, Med-bay is behind the snack bar?"

"Haven't you noticed the back wall is a bit thick between here and the theater?"

"Well, yes, but I thought it was storage."

"Of a sort."

They went into the enclosed snack bar and through another door in the back, which opened to a gleaming metal and white medical facility. Two flat tables with plexiglass tubes took up half the room. The other half had two chairs and a variety of shelves and drawers.

"So, if you want to understand our culture, you'll need to take a memory-cube and download it through these lenses." Sol took a glowing green cube out of one of the drawers and a pair of weird-looking metal glasses from another. He hooked a cord to the cube, attached it to the sunglasses, and waved to one of the chairs. "You'll want to sit down. It's pretty disorientating, and you might even want to strap in." He indicated the seatbelt on the chair.

Amaya wasn't ready to accept anything else disorientating before she had some of her questions answered. "Before I do this, I want to know about what your aunt meant earlier, about the 'fight' you had."

Sol sighed. "It would really be easier if you would download the memory-cube first."

"No. Tell me something first about the situation we're in. What happened and why did the theater… ship take off so quickly? How did you know those ships were in Earth's orbit?"

"While you were watching your movie, a handful of Ratterran spies dressed as Earthers came to the theater. They were looking for us, well, for a specific Terr, actually. They didn't find who they were looking for, but we weren't able to stop them before they reported our presence to their patrol ships, which were cloaked in Earth's orbit."

"And you fought them?"

"Yes." He nodded.

"But they didn't land any blows on you?"

"Well, one of them tore my uniform with his blade, but I was able to defend myself before he did any real damage."

"Good." Amaya dipped her head. "I mean, I'm glad Ratterrans obviously don't fight as well as I do. I'll have a chance if I meet any."

"What do you mean?"

"Well, they weren't able to land any blows on you, but I did." She grinned at him.

He rolled his eyes. "I wasn't expecting an Earther to be as fast as you or as strong as you. You got lucky."

"I don't believe in luck."

"Fine. You got me. They didn't. But don't underestimate Ratterrans. They're devious and full of deceit."

"Isn't that the same thing?"

"No." His furrowed brow made a wrinkle in his forehead. It was kind of cute, but Amaya forced herself to look away. She wasn't sure she could trust him. The way he'd held her back from the door still didn't seem right.

Amaya stepped back. "How do I know you're the good guys?"

JUST TRUST ME

"Just trust me, please." Sol turned on his sexy, charming voice again. His deep green eyes gazed at her in a soulful way. It probably worked on most girls, but Amaya's temper sparked at the sound of the velvety fakeness in his voice.

"Why would I trust you? I still don't know anything about you."

Sol squinted and held up his hand. "Sorry. Please, just remain calm. You can trust my aunt. She's a captain of the Terr Royal Space Force, ranked at the top of her class at the Academy. She's a Rover Captain, special intelligence for the royal family, working to clean up our messes. It wasn't her planned career move, but she met my uncle. They fell in love, which made everyone in their families unhappy."

"Classic Romeo and Juliet, but with no death, so maybe more like Cinderella?" She loved comparing stories to real-life situations. The comparisons made life more manageable, like a narrative with defined points and a purpose.

"Do both of those stories involve talking mice?"

"What? No." Amaya rolled her eyes. "All right. I'll do this memory-cube thing, but you seriously have to learn more Earth culture when you have a chance."

He dipped his head and stared down at the ground. "If you say so, I will." He held out the glasses.

She took them, not sure what to make of his change of attitude. "Thanks." She sat in the chair. "I get that I put these over my eyes, but how does any of this work with human biochemistry?"

"Terrs have traveled The Great Galaxy for hundreds of Earther years. Our scientists have discovered ways for many peoples to use the same technology. For now, you need to help the cube understand your biochemistry and activate it by holding it in your hands." He held the cube out, too.

"Finally, an explanation that kind of makes sense." Amaya put the weird glasses on, and the room darkened. She held out her hands for the cube, and he guided her fingers around it. For a moment, nothing happened, and he held her hands in his. It was almost—

The world dropped out, down, and away. She was swept into a swirl of colors, images, sounds, smells, tastes, textures, oceans of knowledge and experience. Children laughed. Grandparents swam in the sea. Fields, floods, mountains, seas, skies, a royal lineage, war, seas again.

As quickly as the experience started, it stopped. Amaya understood what the juice comment meant now. She thought he was wrong, but she wasn't offended by it. She sat there for a moment, feeling thoroughly stunned. Then the cube dropped from her fingers and tumbled to the floor by her chair.

Where is Sol?

With a tumble of images, she suddenly knew why her vow earlier had been taken so seriously, why Sol had reacted the way he had to her demand of him to understand more of Earth culture. He hadn't just apologized and asked for forgiveness. No, he'd taken it a thousand steps further by giving his life to her as a Bond. The Bond would last until he died as her guardian, or until she accepted him as her mate and restored his honor with marriage.

What in The Great Galaxy had he been thinking?

The Great Galaxy, that was the name the Terr and other cultures gave to both the Milky Way Galaxy and their spiritual connection with it. Some referred to The Great Galaxy as Xia, like people on Earth used the expression Gaia. Other people deferred to the Triple One, a triune deity which reminded Amaya of Earth Christianity, the belief system she'd been raised with by her parents. *Are they the same?* They were similar, for sure. Then there was the Rayatana, a friend of the stars, a prophesied Child of Three Worlds. The Rayatana would reunite The Great Galaxy under one rule or she would destroy them all. Opinions on that varied, too.

She put her hand to her head. *What's going on?* All that information streaming into her consciousness; it was the memory-cube. Every question she had about The Great Galaxy had some form of short answer in a pathway in her head now, and it felt amazing.

Still, she just wanted to go home.

And she wanted to fix this problem with Sol. By accepting his Bond, by saying she'd honor it and hold him to his Word, she'd practically betrothed herself to him. *Why had Geral and Prya allowed me to do that?* They had to know she didn't understand. *There was no way I could be held responsible for words I didn't understand, right?* Except, she could be. That rush of heat and emotion, that was what the memory-cube told her was "Sign of Zoe or a Zoe Bond." Zoe meant life, specifically, soul life. *How can I be bonded that way to an alien dude I don't know that well?*

This was not good, not fair. She had to find him and find a way to undo what she'd inadvertently done.

She took off the dark glasses and squinted against the light of the Med-lab.

How long was I in the cube?

WARNING

Warning sirens, like the ones she'd heard earlier, broke the quiet of Med-bay.

She jumped out of the chair and started toward the doorway.

Sol entered, and they collided. Amaya lost her balance, but he steadied her with one hand on her shoulder. "I'm sorry, Amaya. I…" He stared down at her, pressed his lips together, and then sighed. "We have to go before the Ratterrans find us."

At the word "Ratterrans," images jumbled through Amaya's mind, like an encyclopedia download. The Ratterrans had been at war with the Terrs for a thousand years, ever since both cultures had fought over the Ganyth System, one of the more lucrative trading systems in the galaxy due to the minerals needed for space travel.

"There's a hidden escape hatch in here, behind the hydroponics cabinet with our herbal supplies."

Sol stepped past Amaya into the Med-bay and walked over to a tall cabinet. He opened one of the doors to reveal a mini hydroponics area, with herbs growing in small containers. He reached toward the back of the cabinet, and it swung open to reveal another small hatch behind it.

Amaya glanced out into the snack booth beyond the Med-bay. She couldn't see Prya or Geral. "What about your aunt and uncle? Aren't they coming?"

"They're buying us time." He held out his hand. "Are you coming?"

She bit her lip. Everything had been happening so fast. She didn't understand the situation, even with the culture download she'd received. The sirens blared on repeat, and Sol continued to hold out his hand, but she froze with indecision.

Laser fire melted the snack booth windows and hit the popcorn machine right outside the doorway. Amaya yelped and shut the door. She raced across the Med-bay. Ignoring Sol's hand, she climbed through the hatch into a tiny hallway.

"To the right. Quietly."

Amaya nodded and turned to the right, keeping her steps small and fast. When she reached another hatch, presumably leading outside, she paused.

Sol was right behind her. He pushed a button on the side of the hatch, and the door slid open. A blast of wintry wind hit Amaya in the face, and she shivered. She wasn't dressed for weather like this. She glanced at Sol, who wore his dorky, ripped movie theater uniform.

Even worse than the cold, though, was that the open hatch revealed a long drop to the ground.

Sol hit another button, and a drawer opened by the door. Climbing gear, backpacks with supplies, she hoped, and helmets sat inside the open compartment.

"We're always prepared for anything," Sol said. "The bulkhead on the other side has a life raft."

Amaya nodded. She had entered into a state of fight-*and*-flight. It wasn't one or the other. She was taking the situation as it came, and doing whatever was needed, as her mom had taught her to do for years.

Sol handed her a harness and a backpack before putting on his own harness and backpack. He clipped a lead rope into the side of the hatchway, where a ring was built into the ship. Then he clipped himself, and then her, onto the rope.

Amaya was glad she'd rock climbed once with her mom, but once was certainly not enough experience for climbing down a rope from a spaceship to an alien planet. Sol checked her gear. He was business-like and efficient. For the first time, Amaya felt something different than annoyance or attraction toward him. *Respect?* He seemed to know what he was doing, and he was calm in a stressful situation.

But why hasn't anyone come after us? She glanced at Sol. "Do you think your aunt and uncle drew them away from us?"

"I closed the hydroponics unit. Unless you know where to look, the hatch should remain hidden." He glanced down at the long drop. Then back at her. "Your gear has a safety stop." He showed her where this was on her ascender. This one appeared more high-tech than the usual earth climbing gear. Like the ones she had used before, though, it was a simple press of the button to clamp down on the rope so she wouldn't freefall to the ground.

"Ready?"

She wasn't, but what choice did she have?

LET ME GO

"Let me go first." Sol turned his back to the open hatch and glanced down at her. "I'll do my best to slow our descent."

"Are you saying you'll catch me if I fall?" Amaya asked, feeling a nervous giggle bubbling up inside her chest.

His lips quirked, as if he were going to tease her.

The whole ship jolted, and he held fast to the sides of the open hatch. "We have to go now." He stepped out of the hatch and began descending, using the ascender clip to break every foot or so.

Amaya watched for a moment. Taking a deep breath, she climbed out of the hatch and leaned against her rope. Her heart pounded in her chest. The air was freezing on her legs, her arms, and her face. She gripped the rope tight, with one hand on the rope and another on the ascender. She forced herself to stare out at the horizon line, stepped out, and let go.

The freezing air shocked her even more as she braked for the first time, then slipped, then braked. She was actually doing this; dangling above an alien landscape of purple trees and orange brush, rappelling out of a spaceship. She forced herself to breathe every time she braked. It was slow going, but steady. Terrifying. She looked up to see the ship was farther away. She looked down and clenched in fear. Her hand clutched the brake in a death grip.

"Amaya? Are you all right?" Sol's voice came up from beneath her.

She nodded before realizing he couldn't see her.

"I...I'll be okay." She squeezed her eyes shut, inhaled again, and let it out. She prayed, not a coherent prayer, but a quick cry of her heart.

When she opened her eyes, she stared out at the yellow tree trunks, straight out in front of her. The tops of those trees were holding up the spaceship above her. They were strong. She could be strong, too. She took a breath again, let the brake loose for a second, and closed it.

Breath.

Word of prayer.

Loosen the brake.

Close it.

And repeat.

After what felt like an eternity, something bumped against her feet. She glanced down.

Sol stood on the snowy ground, holding her feet in his hands. "I'm here. You're safe."

She eased out the brake again, slid to the ground, and leaned against him.

He held her tight against his chest and brushed his lips against her forehead. Her heart pounded in her ears. *I'm definitely falling for an alien dude on an alien planet.*

MAYBE

Maybe I can trust Sol.

Maybe I can survive this crazy adventure after all.

She leaned into him for several minutes, breathing in rhythm with him, listening to his heart. He was like a rock in a storm, a safe haven, at least for the moment. Even if it was his fault she was on an alien planet with Ratterrans after them.

With that thought, she pushed away from him.

The moment was over.

But he still had his arms around her.

She looked up and his jade green eyes with gold specks mesmerized her.

He parted his full lips and leaned toward her, but she shook her head. "No!" She pushed away from him again, this time breaking out of the circle of his arms. "No, I won't be tricked by some alien player on a strange planet with Ratterrans chasing us. This isn't some stupid movie."

"Alien player? What's a 'player'?"

"Someone who plays with people as if it's a game. I'm not going to get played," she informed him. "Besides, aren't we running for our lives?" She pointed up at the ship.

"Yes, but you need to trust me and trust I'm not playing you like a game. I…didn't mean to offend you." He gazed at her with puppy dog eyes.

"Let's get out of here, go someplace safe." She turned her back on him while unclipping herself from the rope, and then she removed her climbing harness.

"There's a settlement five clicks in one direction and another ten clicks away. I think we should go to the one farther away, but it will be a tough trek."

"To throw them off our trail, we're going to go farther? You have noticed I'm not dressed for this cold, right?" She faced him as she said this.

"Yes." His gaze roamed up and down her body.

"That wasn't an invitation to check me out!" *Boys were so rude. It doesn't seem to matter what planet they're from. I'm smarter than this.* She'd been hurt once before, but once was enough.

"Oh, sorry." His face reddened. "I was seeing if you would fit the coveralls in the emergency kits." He took off his backpack and rummaged through it. "If you check yours, you should find a one-size coverall for all-weather."

She rolled her eyes and pulled off her backpack, not needing a reminder of her short stature. Opening up her backpack, she found a loose-fitting garment inside. It was definitely too tall for her, but warmth would be better than nothing. She stepped into it and tried to figure out the closing mechanism — was it a metal Velcro?

Sol walked to her, with his coverall already over his ridiculous uniform. His coverall fit him perfectly. He held out his hands. "May I? There's a way to adjust it."

"Okay, but watch your hands."

The redness on his face deepened. "I'll be careful." He pointed to the sides by her waist. "Hold it closed there, and I'll show you the suit controls on the sleeve."

She held the garment closed and watched while he pressed one of the buttons on her sleeve. The suit closed and gathered together. It wasn't her size, but it was definitely more fitted than it had been.

"If you press the red button, it will get warmer inside. The blue makes it colder. The gray one is for camouflage." He pressed this button on his suit, and it turned a combination of purple, yellow, orange, and white. "The other buttons are for health checks and water. There's a pouch of nutrients in the pant leg. I don't recommend eating it unless you have to."

"Noted." She touched the red button, and the suit's material warmed up. Then she touched the gray button and watched how the suit matched the colors of the trees, the bushes, and the snow. Sol had left his climbing helmet on, so she did, too. "Do we need to keep the helmets?"

He shrugged. "You never know what we're going to run across."

She nodded. "Okay. Let's take the long road home."

"There isn't a road."

"It's an expression."

He started walking through the trees. "Earthers, especially English speakers, have too many expressions. How do you ever understand each other?"

She matched his steps as best as she could. He was taller, but she was used to having to keep up with tall people. "I take it your download on Earth culture wasn't as complete as mine was about Terr."

14

NO

"No, probably not." Sol held a tree branch aside for Amaya. "I don't understand half of the things you say and the slang isn't…well, it's not what I was expecting."

"What were you expecting?" Amaya knew from her quick download of Terr culture that she didn't understand everything about his culture, but he had been on Earth for several months, living in Washington longer than she had.

He shrugged. "Groovy. Dig it. Far out."

Amaya snorted. "You're stuck in the flower child era."

"The what? I didn't think Earthers had much in common with Dryadarians."

She laughed. "No, no." She snorted, imagining one of her teachers as an Azalea bush with eyes. "I don't mean an actual flower child. It's—"

"An expression?" Sol shook his head. "How

in The Great Galaxy can you communicate with each other? It's as if you purposely confuse everything. No wonder Earth has so much division, so much war. If you had clearer languages, you could understand one another."

The laughter went out of Amaya in a moment, replaced by cold hollowness as memories of her parents' shouting matches returned — the crying, the screaming, the nastiness, and her dad's threats of reporting her mom's immigration status, which still didn't make sense. Her mom had grown up in Washington state. Shivering, she refocused on the here and now.

She wished the warm coverall extended over her feet. Her sneakers were getting wet in the snow. Under these purple trees with orange trunks, she hoped she wasn't being exposed to something unhealthy. *But who am I kidding? I'm on an alien planet, talking to an alien boy, on the run from other aliens.* Except they weren't running. *Why aren't we going faster?*

"Amaya, did I say something wrong again?" Sol's hand brushed her fingers.

"No." She jerked away from him. "I'm wondering why we aren't hurrying to get away from those Ratterrans, and if there's something you're not telling me. Like how my words earlier to your aunt meant much more than I realized? You know, not explaining something, or not saying something, is as bad as using slang? It's worse, because it means you're purposefully hiding the truth."

Sol sighed, and then he glanced back the way they had come. "Even though the Ratterrans shot at you in the Med-bay entrance, the door to the hidden hallway is coded to those with my family's genetics. By not running, our movement is less noticeable under the tree cover and we conserve our energy for the long road." He quirked his lips into a smile, but he let that go when she didn't smile back.

He stopped, held up his hands in front of him, as if in prayer, and opened them like a book. "On my honor, as a Terr and a follower of the Word, I did not mean you harm, not earlier and not now. I'm sorry I did not speak up when you said you would hold me to my Word and my Bond."

"You just let girls vow their lives to yours that easily?"

"No, I didn't think it would be taken seriously since you did not understand what you were saying in our language."

"And you said Earthers don't communicate well?"

He ducked his head and pressed his lips together. "I apologize, Amaya. Will you forgive me?"

"Will you hold me to the vow?"

"No." His face fell, and he gazed at the ground.

She felt bad for pushing him, but she had to know.

"Will your Aunt Prya or Uncle Geral hold me to the vow?"

He ran his hand through his hair, but he didn't look at her. "They will try. I really am sorry, Amaya. I am in your debt. You have my life in your hands." He held out his hands again. "Please, forgive me."

She gazed at his long fingers—tapered and calloused at the ends. They were different, alien, but they were trembling. She placed her hands on either side of his in the formal Terr way. "I forgive you."

15

OVERCOME

Overcome by the gentle warmth of Sol's hands under hers, Amaya closed her eyes, letting herself enjoy the moment. Forgiveness felt like a lightening of her soul, as if a heavy slab she'd been carrying was lifted away. She took a deep breath, held it, and then let it out before sending up another quick prayer.

Opening her eyes, she glanced up at Sol.

He gazed at her with his eyes half-lidded. His pupils were wide.

She stepped back from him again. Even if she forgave him, even if she was drawn to him, connected to him in a way she didn't understand, it didn't mean she trusted him completely. "So, how much farther do we need to go?"

He clicked a button on his watch and furrowed his brow. "Nine clicks. We have a long way to go for… the long road home."

He was trying to use one of her expressions. He

meant well, so she flashed him a smile. "Okay. Let's get going. Why don't you tell me about your family while we walk? Why are Ratterrans after you? The cube didn't exactly cover the topic. I know you've been at war for several generations, but why did they attack you on Earth? Why now?"

"I don't know where to start." He pressed his lips together and started walking through the purple trees with the yellow bark again, winding a path through the undergrowth. She walked with him, patient for the moment. At least he was planning on answering her questions.

"Ratterrans have looked for ways to usurp the Terr Rulership for several generations, but in the last twenty years, they have been more subtle. Assassins in court, spies embedded everywhere. It is hard to know who to trust." He glanced at her.

She quirked an eyebrow like Spock in *Star Trek*™. It was one of her nerdiest accomplishments. "You think I'm a Ratterran spy? That is highly illogical."

He gave her a funny look, as if trying to interpret her tone of voice. "No. It's hard to talk about it. I hope you'll understand."

"I still want a few details."

"My aunt and uncle went to Earth on a mission to find and protect someone from our family who'd gone missing. I was sent to live with them some cycles ago. I had embarrassed my family and was meant to aid them in their…work."

"What did you do?"

He kicked at a lump of snow, and it broke apart. "It's pretty embarrassing, but it didn't happen the way everyone thought it did. There was this girl…"

"Mm-hmm." Amaya raised her eyebrows.

"It isn't…it wasn't…I didn't…" His face flushed, and he held up his hands. "Just listen. She was from another noble family, and she wanted an alliance. Actually, her father wanted an alliance with my family. I just thought she wanted to get out of the stuffy formal dinners and go sea-skating. She was disappointed when I brought a bunch of friends, and she couldn't get me alone, but she tried to tell everyone that I…I charmed her." He ran a hand through his hair.

"You mean charmed like convinced her with pretty words? How is charming a big deal?"

"No, like this." In three words, his voice dropped, purred for a moment, and then went up again.

Amaya tilted her head. "You have some kind of voice power?"

"I'm supposed to have the power to charm. It's a Terr trait. I have a little extra speed, a little extra strength, and not enough charm to even charm an Earth girl."

"You mean me?"

"Yeah." He peered at the ground.

"Interesting." She pieced together what he'd told her with the information she'd gained from the memory-cube. "Are Terrs the only ones with these powers?"

"No. The charm and other powers used to be spread out throughout all the people on our planet, and all the planets in our solar system."

"But Ratterrans don't believe in powers?"

"Ratterrans…" He shook his head. "I don't understand them. They say they want the power to rule themselves without relying on anything but their mechanized science. They say they want to be left alone, but they have destroyed so many of my people. They hunt us down, even on Earth."

"So, you didn't tell me everything earlier to protect the missing Terr?"

"Yes."

Amaya thought this over as she walked a few more steps with him. "All right. Let's say I believe your stories. Why did Ratterrans attack the movie theater-spaceship? Were they after you and your aunt and uncle?"

Sol stopped walking and put his finger to his lips.

Amaya stilled, listening.

A low rumbling sound came from overhead.

He backed into the trunk of a tree and held out his hands.

She stepped toward him, allowing him to hold her close as they peered through the tree's canopy.

Above them, a small ship flew in the same direction they had been walking. A heavy droning sound signaled the approach of a larger spaceship, flying low. The movie-theater spaceship followed close behind, with a beam of light connecting it to the two ships like a tow cable.

When the ships receded into the distance, Sol gazed at Amaya. "My aunt and uncle must have been taken. If the ship is under Ratterran control, I need to save them."

"Well, I guess it's good we're already walking in the right direction then."

"Thank you." He smiled broadly.

She grinned back. "You're welcome. But let's get going, okay?" She stepped out into the open area between the trees.

PULSING BEAMS OF LIGHT

Pulsing beams of light split the yellow tree trunk next to Amaya.

She screamed and ducked into a roll. Continuing the motion to her feet again, she bent low and ran behind another tree. Her heart pounded in her chest. Her martial arts instructor would have been proud of her defensive roll.

She glanced around for Sol and another hiding place, knowing she couldn't stay in one spot for long but also not wanting to get the shooter's attention.

What will I do on a strange planet if Sol is killed or taken?

Thankfully, she glimpsed a bit of Sol's hair between a clump of trees growing out of a nursery trunk in a fallen tree. She plotted a course to him in two maneuvers and started toward her first stop.

A pulse beam hit the ground next to her. She threw herself to the other side, launched forward, and hid behind another tree trunk. The pulse beams hit the ground where she'd been, as well as the tree trunk on the opposite side of where she hid. They knew where she was.

How am I going to survive this?

Sol poked his head up and shot a weapon at them. No light emitted from his tiny gun, but a blast hit something. "Come on. I'll cover you," he shouted.

Amaya nodded, glanced to the side, and went toward a copse of trees before zigging left behind the nursery log. She slid across mucky dirt and slush in an effort to stay low.

Sol continued shooting the small weapon he held. It didn't look like any gun Amaya had ever seen, more like a phaser from a science fiction show her mom liked.

"Here." Sol handed her a weapon like his. "This is a grenjen."

Amaya took the slender, short rod in her hands. It had recessed buttons on the top.

"Point that end and shoot," Sol said, indicating the tapered end.

"Got it." Amaya held the weapon carefully in her hand, not aiming at either of them.

Pulses of light slammed into the nursery log. Splinters flew around them.

"Now!"

Kneeling next to him, she gripped the weapon in her hand, but she didn't shoot.

Their attackers had taken cover behind a set of boulders.

Sol fired his weapon, and an energy blast hit the boulders with a crack, shattering pieces of rock. Dark scores in the rock showed Sol's previous hits.

Amaya bit her lip. *Can I kill someone?*

A pulse beam hit the nursery log, and she ducked, sucking back a scream. They weren't giving her a choice.

The next time Sol stood, she stood, too, and fired her weapon before he fired his. The recoil was minimal, which surprised her. She fired again and again, going for the edges of the rock because she couldn't see their attackers.

Sol put his hand on her arm. "Fire once, wait two counts, fire again, wait three counts. We'll have a better chance of hitting them, and the grenjen won't run out of energy."

Amaya nodded.

One of their attackers poked his head out from behind the rock.

Sol shot at the Ratterran, and the alien fell back into undergrowth.

Amaya held her grenjen at the ready, but no one else looked out from around the boulder.

Several minutes passed, and the forest became eerily silent around them.

QUIET

"Quiet." Amaya whispered to Sol when a small branch snapped underneath him.

A pulse beam shot around the rock, angled off, and hit a tree to the left of them.

Amaya ducked behind the nursery log.

Sol stayed upright and fired again. Then he crouched next to her.

"How many?" Amaya said.

"Two more. We could shimmy through that and come out the other side…" He pointed to an opening in the nursery log.

Amaya glanced into the log. It was hollow inside, and they could fit, but a mound of something on the other end had a rank smell. "I think something has a nest in there."

"Let me see." Sol leaned across her and peered into the hollow log. He touched his watch, and a ray of light pierced the darkness inside. Something moved at the other end. "Nardels. Not good. Not good." He sat back and pulled Amaya with him. "We have to get away from this opening."

A low growl emanated from the log.

A pulse beam crashed into the other side of it.

"Now." Sol sprang to his feet, shot carelessly toward the boulder, and grabbed Amaya by the arm. "Toward the Ratterans!"

"What?" Amaya shouted.

The growling grew louder inside the log, and she understood.

They ran toward the boulder, firing wildly at it as they went.

Amaya glanced back. Behind them, something huge, with yellow and purple fur, clawed its way out of the nursery log. The claws on the creature were as long as her arms. The elongated, red snout revealed fangs. She turned back to the boulder, firing again.

Sol dove to the side where the Ratterran had fallen, and she followed him, but in a crouch. Sol fired behind the boulder.

Amaya aimed at the female Ratterran fiddling with her weapon. The other two Ratterrans, both male, were down in the undergrowth, dead from their wounds.

"Drop it!" Amaya shouted at the Ratterran woman.

She curled her lip in disdain, showing off a high-ranking tooth jewel, and dove for Amaya.

Amaya side-stepped and fired at her leg.

The woman screamed.

"Nice work. Let's go." Sol grabbed at Amaya's arm again.

"Knock it off!" Amaya yanked her arm away from him. "I don't like being dragged around. And I'm not leaving her to fend off that thing." She spun and took aim at the snarling creature leaping across the clearing toward them.

"No!"

One clean shot to its chest and it went down in a screech. It raised its head and whimpered. Amaya shot it again.

The creature died.

She turned to Sol. "What is wrong with you?" She'd lost trust in him again. *How could anyone decent leave someone to die under the claws of an angry beast?*

"She had young in her nest. The Nardels, though deadly, are necessary for the survival of the forests on this planet. The young will not survive without their mother."

"And what of this woman? Will her children

survive without her?" Amaya pointed at the Ratterran, who glared at her as she pressed her hand against the blackened wound on her shattered leg.

"I would rather die than rot in your prisons. I will tell you nothing," the Ratterran growled in the Terr language.

"You are nothing, Ratterran scum," Sol retorted, with his face contorted in anger. He raised his weapon.

"No! I won't go a step farther with you if you shoot her," Amaya informed him.

"You care more for a Ratterran who was trying to kill you than you do for the mother of cubs? Besides, if we leave her here, she will call her Ratterran friends, and they will come after us."

"Then we take her communications system, call for help from a third party, and get a ride to the spaceport. The Ratterran, the Nardel young, and us."

"What?!" Sol shook his head. "No. That is not possible."

"Really? Or you just don't like my plan?"

The Ratterran laughed, and then she whimpered in pain. "He…is a Terr…his way is without mercy. He…would rather die than surrender. As would I. It is our way." She put her wrist to her mouth, tore a container off the side of her bracelet, and swallowed it.

"Poison," Sol said.

"No." Amaya knelt next to the woman as she shook. When she died, Amaya lowered the woman's eyelids. Swaying under the gravity of the death dealt around them, some by her own hand, Amaya gazed at the Ratterran's bracelet. It held a medallion with a familiar symbol on it, much like the shooting star on the back of Amaya's necklace. With a glance, she noticed Sol was looking at one of the other Ratterrans. *Good.* She rested her hand over the bracelet, undid the clasp with her fingers, and cupped the bracelet in her hand. She needed a closer inspection of it, without Sol around. *I don't want him to see what I noticed. Not yet.*

"What are you doing?" Sol leaned closer.

"Putting her to rest." Amaya crossed the woman's hands over her chest, noticing for the first time how short and blunt the woman's fingers were in contrast to her own fingers and, especially Sol's long, thin fingers. Very little separated their species. And yet, so much cultural conditioning separated the Ratterran and the Terr peoples. She didn't understand.

"She's a soldier. She doesn't expect to rest." He knelt down by Amaya and glared down at the woman's body. "She knew what it meant to attack a Terr."

Amaya leaned away from him and stared down at the woman's face. "If I had acted sooner, I could have saved her. And your idea to leave her behind to be eaten by a wild animal, endangered or not… I don't understand how you can do something like that to an injured intelligent person." She drew a shaky breath and got to her feet. "She's dead because of us. I killed the first Ratterran to save myself. But this woman, she died because of my lack of swift action and your cold disregard for life." Bile rose to her throat and an ache grew in her chest. She stumbled away from the Ratterran bodies.

Sol reached out for her.

"Don't touch me!"

REVIEW

"Amaya, I… it hurts when you're angry with me." Sol had his hand to his chest.

She felt the same pain. *Was it the Zoe Bond? Would it do that to them?* Images from the memory-cube flickered in her mind. *Yes. The Zoe Bond can cause pain.* She shook her head at Sol and continued to walk away from him, despite the ache. She needed to think.

Review and reassess. Those words repeated in Amaya's head as she moved away from Sol, toward the dead Nardel and the nursery log. Amaya's mom had often rebuked her with that repeated phrase when she made mistakes. *Review and reassess.* Her dad had hated the phrase, had disliked how her mom had signed Amaya up for martial arts, wilderness training, and archery. Yet, Amaya had loved and excelled at all of it, despite her mom pushing them on her. On the other hand, her dad understood her dance and gymnastics classes, but he'd never wanted to see her excel at anything defensive or aggressive. She wished she knew why her dad wanted one thing for her and her mom wanted another. After the divorce, her dad had distanced himself from both of them, and it hurt. *Why?*

But, thinking of that isn't going to help me now. I have to shove it aside. What do I know of myself? Of this situation?

"Amaya?" Sol's inquiry hung in the air.

"Just let me think," she said without looking back. She would start with reviewing him first. It would be easier than looking at herself.

What do I know about Sol? He was a good-looking alien guy who worked at the movie theater, which was actually a spaceship. He was a Terr, from the royal Terr line. His aunt was the captain of her own movie-theater ship. His uncle was estranged from the royal family but continued to do their bidding. They had been on Earth to find a missing Terr royal, when Ratterran spies attacked them. Which led them to escape to this planet, where they crash-landed, and they gave Amaya a memory-cube of information that lacked information about Ratterrans, other than the fact that they were the enemy.

But who was on the right side of The Thousand Years' War between the two cultures, led by two families who had once been bonded in rulership over their planetary system? The memory-cube had withheld details about why the two families and cultures had separated. Was Sol actually the good guy in this situation? He was willing to leave a Ratterran woman for the Nardel, and he obviously viewed her as less important than a creature of the forest. He knew more than Amaya did in this situation, but his view was skewed by his culture and his family. Some of his "help" was grabby, bossy help.

Can I trust Sol? He had saved her several times from death, and she had to credit him for those actions. He was also in her debt. That was to her advantage as well. He hadn't shot the Ratterran woman when she told him not to, or at least he had hesitated. These things were all in his favor. But she couldn't trust him to treat everyone with basic decency, which was a problem.

She worried at her necklace through the coveralls as she walked slowly past the dead Nardel to the Nardel's den. When she was close to the nursery log, she looked back at Sol. He was bending over one of the Ratterran bodies.

She moved partially behind the nursery log and peered inside. Tiny mewling sounds and small movements showed her the location of the Nardel young in their nest. She wondered if they could be saved, if someone on this planet would care for them.

Thinking of this, she slid her necklace out from under her shirt and compared the shooting star symbol on the back with the symbol on the bracelet she had taken from the Ratterran woman. They were the same. The exact same. Right then, she realized she had seen the other symbol on the back of her necklace all day long — the three stars in a triangular formation. They were on the one-piece suit she wore, except the symbol on the coveralls had been stylized with lines between the three stars. Although they were slightly different, they still matched.

Why are those symbols on my necklace? What does it mean?

Feeling dizzy with confusion, she slumped down to the snow-covered ground by the Nardel nest and listened to their mewling. She was just as lost as they were.

Why are the symbols of the Terr and Ratterran peoples doing on the back of my necklace? And, what does the symbol of intertwined ovals on the front mean?

She didn't know.

Review and reassess.

The repetition of the words usually comforted her, but she had more questions than answers, and she didn't trust Sol with her questions. *Would he treat me with contempt if he knew about my necklace?* She had always thought her upbringing was different. Her mom had wanted her to be able to defend herself, but today she'd found out she was trained as a soldier in a war she hadn't even known existed.

Who am I? Who is my mom? Who were my grandparents?

SUNSET

Sunset on this planet was strange. The blue sky turned gold, not purple over the purple-hued forest. Somehow the strangeness comforted her, reminded her that she wasn't home. Surely some of the unsettled feelings she had could be blamed on being on an alien planet.

Despite the strangeness, she appreciated the beauty of the sunset. The wind picked up, rustling through the tree tops, creating the sound of waves on an ocean shore. Amaya was thankful her coveralls were warm.

Sol had used one of the communicators on the Ratterran woman to call a transport driver while Amaya checked on the Nardel nest. After the call, he stayed quiet, respecting Amaya's need for silence.

The transport arrived before full dark. It was a flying, boxy vehicle with three compartments: one for the driver, one for passengers, and one for cargo.

The pilot of the vehicle—an alien man with

green skin, leaves in his hair, and tiny flower buds growing out of his ear lobes where Amaya would expect earrings—rolled down his window a crack to speak to them when he arrived.

"Tell me again why I should not call our security forces, Terr."

"These Ratterrans attacked us. We defended ourselves," Sol said, holding out his hands, which were currently weaponless.

Amaya wondered for a moment why she could understand the alien driver's speech, and then a bit of information came to her, courtesy of the memory-cube download. She understood four languages now— English, Terr, Galaxy Trade Tongue also known as Xiatat, and Dryadarian. The driver was a Dryadarian, a tree in human form.

"And what do you say?" The Dryadarian looked pointedly at Amaya.

She sighed. "It is as he says, although the Ratterran woman poisoned herself when I thought we could take her captive."

The Dryadarian driver's skin changed from dark green to pale green, and he shook his head. "It is the way of The Thousand Years' War, a way of violence without end until the prophesied Rayatana comes." He closed his eyes. "May these people's roots become the seeds of the next generation. May they see life in the everlasting. So be it."

"Amen," Amaya said and glanced at Sol.

"So be it." His words came out slow and reluctant, and his lips twisted on the last word.

The Dryadarian pressed some controls in the transport, and the doors on the cargo area opened. "If you will carefully place the Nardels in the cage, I will take care of the bodies of the Ratterrans. I will not leave them here to mingle with the soil of an alien planet."

Amaya thought she understood what he meant, and she was glad of it. These Ratterrans had families, presumably, who would want to know what had happened to them, and to have a chance to mourn them. She put her hand to her heart and dipped her head toward the Dryadarian.

His eyes widened, but he repeated the symbolic gesture for respect. "Thank you." He glanced at Sol. "If you will see to the Nardels?"

"I'll need your help," Sol said to Amaya.

She nodded. "Okay." She walked with him toward the nest. When they were farther away, the Dryadarian driver got out of the vehicle, glancing at them as he did so. Apparently, he didn't trust Sol, either.

Moving the Nardels meant working closely with Sol, but she didn't know what to say.

Sol produced a vial from his pack, opened it,

and threw it into the log by the nest. "It will put them to sleep so we can move them."

After a moment, the whimpering sounds of the Nardel young ceased. Sol leaned into the main part of the log and tugged the nest out. Together, they picked up the nest of the sleeping Nardel babies and carried it to the transport.

Amaya caught Sol's glances in her direction, but she didn't give him a chance to speak to her, always looking at the Nardel babies, who were cuter than anything predatory should be, with their red snouts curled under their giant paws.

Finally, they had the nest secured safely in the cage in the cargo area. The other side held the Ratterrans' bodies, all laid carefully on a tarp.

The Dryadarian was back in his pilot's cab, separated from them.

Sol opened the door to the passenger seating area and waited for Amaya to get inside.

She slid into the cab, thankful for the two separate seats, one facing forward and one facing backward. The windows had bars over them, and a barred window separated them from the front compartment and the back compartment. The inside wasn't plush. The seat's frayed fabric wasn't something Amaya was familiar with. She picked at one of the loose threads and stared out the window.

Once they were in the passenger seating, the driver took off through the woods.

Sol leaned toward her. "We need to find my aunt and uncle's ship. We'll make a plan once we see the situation."

"Research, reconnaissance, plan, then action?" She still didn't look at him but fixed her gaze on the how the forest softened and gave way to open lands of rolling scrub and what looked like gardens.

"Yes." He nodded. "Amaya, may I ask you a question?"

"You just did."

He sighed. "May I ask, how you are…so able to handle everything?"

She turned to glare at him. "I didn't handle those deaths well, if you remember."

He squinted. "You handled it better than some would. Some people, not just Earthers, but beings from all over The Great Galaxy, would not have been able to shoot as you did, would not have remained so calm on the ship, or after the memory-cube download, or on this hard trek to the spaceport. How are you so different?"

Amaya stared down at his knees, which nearly touched hers. She wanted to make light of his questions, to find a sarcastic quip to shut him up, but the reality was, she'd been wondering about those things, too, just as she'd been wondering about the symbols on her necklace. "I don't know."

"Are you sure?"

"My mother made sure I knew how to defend myself. I don't know if there was more to it."

"I see." Sol looked out the windows, away from her.

Is he having as much trouble trusting me as I'm having trouble trusting him? The ache in her chest told her the Zoe Bond was being strained between them. *If I let it control me, I will throw my arms around him, lean into him, but how can I, not knowing who I really am? Or who he really is?*

THE SPACEPORT

The spaceport city bustled with life in every color of the rainbow, and Amaya suspected she couldn't see the full color spectrum with her human eyes. She didn't know what she was expecting, but not everyone in the city was Dryadarian, Terr, or Ratterran. There were aliens she had only heard of in myths, fairy tales, and legends, and some she'd never seen before. She wasn't sure what they were really called and she wasn't going to ask in front of their driver, but some of them looked like dragons of a smallish size, giant birds with colorful plumage, and glowing beings, who were bipedal, but elongated in height. Plus, there were aliens who were smaller than her, some slim and some round, some who looked like she imagined Tolkien's dwarves might, if dwarves carried guns and grenjens instead of axes. She was trying hard not to gape and barely paid attention to the way Sol handled the last exchange with their driver, but she caught him give a generous amount of Xiatat Credits to the driver in exchange for keeping their role in the deaths of the Ratterrans quiet, and to take care of the Nardel.

After the Dryadarian dropped them off at the edge of the trading center, Sol wanted to start on a reconnaissance mission in the spaceport. After a few feet of walking through the market next to the spaceport, though, he gave up as Amaya marveled at everything, from the wild range of people to the variety of goods available in the market. At one point, she stopped in the middle of a busy walkway because she thought she saw a pixie, or something like one, flying into a clothing shop that sold space suits.

Sol tapped her on the shoulder and nodded to an establishment with opaque windows. She followed him. The establishment turned out to be a restaurant with a one-way window view of the city street, and another one-way window looking out on the spaceport. An open kitchen took up the center of the restaurant. Private booths along the walls created seating areas. Once they took a seat, and the booth's privacy doors closed, Amaya gawked openly at the spaceport's hangar. Ships of all sizes and shapes dotted the cavernous space.

"This place is used for illegal trade," Sol explained. "That's why the tables are in individual nooks with opaque glass doors. The windows are one-way, so no one can see inside."

Amaya nodded slowly. "Good."

"You seemed to take our Dryadarian driver in stride, so what is the matter?"

"The number of people." Amaya paused. "I mean, the number of different types of people here. Do I call them 'people'?"

"For some reason, the Elvesan made their word stick for that in the Xiatat language, so we call all intelligent people 'tuigseach.'"

"Tuig…seach?"

"Yes."

Amaya thought it sounded like something from somewhere on Earth, but she wasn't sure. "How, I mean, why…do I recognize so many of these other tuigseach? Elvesan and dragons don't exist anywhere outside fantasy books on Earth How can they be here? Real?" *They were real. And they were aliens.* "Did they visit Earth?"

Sol nodded. "Yes. Over many years of exploration, the people of three systems have visited Earth. Terrs don't cover all the tuigseach in our memory-cube because we use that device in limited fashion and for our own culture."

Amaya bit her lip. Maybe the reason Ratterrans weren't mentioned much in the Terr memory-cube wasn't because of The Thousand Years' War or because of cultural bigotry. Maybe they were left out because most of the tuigseach knew about each other.

I might have misjudged him.

"Each tuigseach has their own memory-cube or memory device. It is not good to take in too many in the same season, and having more information than what we gave you could also be detrimental to your mental health."

"I thought you said it was safe!" She threw up her hands. "What else did you leave out?"

Sol sighed and held his hands together on the table. "It is not the Terr way to divulge everything at once, and, in my defense, I did not know how much you could handle, but I am sorry, Amaya. I truly am. I know you don't understand and the deaths of those Ratterrans hurt you." He put one hand over his chest, and one hand out on the table, palm up. "Please, forgive me."

She nodded, and the tension in her chest lessened. Still, she didn't take his hand. Forgiveness was one thing. Trust was another.

What would he do if he knew about the symbols on my necklace? One thing she knew for sure, she needed him to get home. She didn't know how to resolve their Bond, but she didn't have to let it run her life entirely, either. "Tell me about five tuigseach and point them out to me. Then, tell me your plan. Give me something, at least."

Sol looked down at his hand before withdrawing it.

"There are nine planets in the Terr Protectorate, and each planet is the origin place of at least one tuigseach, with the exception of the Ratterrans. The Ratterrans hold nine planets, as well, but they were once Terr."

"The memory-cube indicated something like that."

"Oh, I had forgotten—"

He was interrupted by a knock on the privacy booth door. Through the glass, Amaya saw a Dryadarian woman with blue-flowering petals covering her head and arms.

Sol glanced at Amaya, and then he opened the door. "We would like two bowls of granchen stew, a loaf of bread, some cheese, and two awaks."

The server took notes on her wristcom, nodded at them, and left.

"Why do I know more from the memory-cube about Dryadarians than the other cultures?"

"They have had the most contact with Terrs than any of the other tuigseach. They are peaceful and have often tried to broker peace between Terrs and Ratterrans. They are highly admired throughout The Great Galaxy for their wisdom, for they are the oldest living tuigseach of all. They feature even in Earth religions."

"What?"

"I don't understand Earth religions that well, but Dryadarians were there, long ago. When humans fell from the Triple One's favor, choosing their own desires, the Triple One sent the Dryadarians to the Faran System, where they rooted near the fourth star."

Amaya put her hands to her head. "I don't know if I can accept that." She stared down at the metal table, then out the window again. "I'm not ready to get into belief systems or the origins of Earth or The Great Galaxy right now. Why don't you tell me about…" She paused to decide on which tuigseach to ask him about. One she didn't recognize came into view. It was bipedal, but strangely thin, with elongated fingers and a head with bulbous eyes. Every bit of the being's skin glowed. "Um, the glowing ones?"

"They have not shared their true name with us. They are called Glowers by most of the tuigseach, and they call each other that in Xiatat, although they seem to think it is an amusing name for themselves. They do not invite anyone to visit their home planet beyond their embassy spaceport. They hold important planets in the neutral zone, in which we are currently hiding. I'm afraid there is little I know of their cultural systems. They are mysterious."

"Why are so many of the tuigseach bipedal?"

Sol shrugged. "There is a pattern, and unless we discuss beliefs or biological origins, I do not think I can go beyond that as an explanation."

Amaya nodded distractedly while staring at the tuigseach in the hangar, working in or around various types of spaceships. Suddenly, she wondered about something Sol had said earlier. "You mentioned Terrs have a lot of contact with Dryadarians. Is this a typical spaceport? Would a spaceport on Terr have so many different tuigseach?"

"No." Sol looked down at his hands resting on the table. "You…challenge many of the things I was raised to think of as normal practices, Amaya. I did not realize an Earther would do that. I did not expect you to be so…open in your thoughts and actions."

Amaya put her hand to her necklace. She wasn't ready to share what she had discovered yet, but the symbols, although confusing, still brought her comfort. "I know that not everyone is accepting or kind to people who are different. I've had to deal with that my whole life. I want to know if it's possible for The Great Galaxy to be different, or if it's something that's messed up beyond Earth."

"While I may have teased you about misunderstandings earlier with your language and slang, the problems with intolerance are throughout The Great Galaxy." He slumped in his seat, with his gaze lowered down.

They sat in silence. Amaya looked out the window, not intruding on Sol's thoughts. *Maybe he can change. Maybe if he can, others can.* She hoped so, as she watched a group of varied tuigseach working together around one of the larger spaceships. It seemed to be a commercial aircraft, and the workers all wore uniform coveralls.

A light knock on their door announced their server, who put a tray of steaming food in the center of their table, nodded politely, and exited without speaking.

"Why didn't she speak to us?"

"In this kind of place, most customers prefer the disturbances to be kept to a minimum."

"So, it's completely private? How do they make sure their patrons aren't doing something terrible behind the closed doors?"

"It depends on the place." Sol put a hand up. "Don't try anything yet." He reached into his coveralls and pulled out a small device. "This will help me check to make sure the food is compatible to our systems."

"Haven't you eaten it before?"

"Yes, but…" The device beeped and turned green. "It's always good to check for poisons in restaurants."

"Um." Amaya wasn't sure how to hide her shock, so she didn't. "Did you do that on Earth, too?"

"Yes. A Terr is always prepared for potential

assassins."

She raised an eyebrow. "And you think this is necessary everywhere?"

"Yes."

"What about when you are at home?"

"Especially there." Sol's gaze was on the food, but his mouth was drawn down, as if he were haunted by a sad memory.

Amaya stared at him as he placed the dishes from the table in front of them. *What kind of horrible life had he had to make him check for poison before every meal?*

Sol set a bowl of steaming stew in front of her and handed her a slice of bread and cheese. "I don't know if you eat meat, so I ordered the vegetarian stew and these options. I hope you like it."

Amaya took a wide spoon from the tray, ignored the other utensils she didn't recognize, and took a small sip of the stew. It tasted like…some kind of melon with vegetables mixed into it. It was odd, but not unpleasant; sweet and savory, and clean on her tongue. Her stomach grumbled in response to it. She took a bite of the bread. The grain wasn't something she was used to, but the texture was right. She ate slowly. She wasn't an adventurous eater, but she was hungry. "How do I know this won't make me sick, since I'm from Earth?"

"It shouldn't. Your biology is compatible

to Terr biology. I don't know why, but I know it is true, and unless you wish to delve into the subject of xenobiology, it's not something I think we should focus on."

"You're right." Amaya thought about the photo-medicine, the memory-cube, and the Terr and Ratterran symbols on her necklace. The food was probably going to be fine. Still, she continued to chew and swallow each bite carefully, just in case she had problems with it, but her stomach seemed fine. The more she ate, the more the flavors became palatable to her as a mixture. She added in the cheese, and eventually, she tried the warm drink Sol poured into cups. "It's like coffee…or strong tea. Or both. Weird. But good."

Sol smiled. "I thought you might like it. I noticed Earthers are obsessed with coffee, and the flavors are compatible. The stimulant is similar, too."

Amaya stopped drinking it. "Are you saying you just gave me alien stimulants?"

"It's not different than coffee. It won't mess with your higher functions. And we need to stay awake. It's been a long day-cycle."

Amaya agreed, but she left the drink alone after that.

"I can't wrap my head around all the tuigseach, but let's talk about the plan."

"I think we need spaceport coveralls and the helmets they use. Then we need to borrow a maintenance truck and act like we are on call to the ship. It's parked at the far end of the hanger, behind you."

Amaya turned in her seat to search for the ship. How had she missed the movie theater-spaceship sitting out there at the edge of the hangar? The Ratterran cruiser was parked next to it. "Okay. But how do we deal with the crew? And don't tell me we're going to kill them all."

Sol swallowed. "I can't promise you anything if there's a fight, but I won't kill them unless there is a threat."

"In self-defense only."

He put his hand to his heart. "In defense only."

She noticed he had left off the "self" part, but she didn't say anything. Their Bond would force him to defend her, even if she tried to make him promise something else. Rubbing her fingers on her necklace, she nodded.

"Amaya? May I ask what symbols are on your necklace? I saw a glint of it earlier. It looked like—"

"I don't want to talk about it right now." She put her hand over her necklace and zipped up her coveralls to her chin. "We can talk about it after we get your aunt, your uncle, and your ship back."

Sol opened his mouth as if to argue, but then he looked away. His hand went to his chest.

Amaya's felt tight, too, but she wasn't going to let the Zoe Bond control her.

IN PLAIN SIGHT

With relative ease, they stole spaceport personnel coveralls, the kind worn by the mechanics and the ground crews, from a maintenance staff locker room. Instead of hiding, they walked in plain sight, wearing the protective helmets equipped with noise cancelling equipment, headsets, and air filters. This all made Sol's plan more viable.

Amaya had doubts, though. She struggled to hide them from Sol. She didn't know what to say to cover her unease, because she wasn't particularly good at telling lies. So, she said as little as possible as they waited for the right moment to "service" the main Ratterran cruiser and retake their theater-spaceship, which according to Sol was a S-Class 29 retrofitted to blend into Earth pop culture.

Finally, a group of Ratterrans left their ship, as well as the other ships, and sauntered into the common area of the spaceport. It was about dinner time, according to Sol. She wasn't sure how much time had passed since she'd been taken from Earth, or how one told time in the galaxy at large, especially with the whole ZIG from solar system to solar system. She felt as though she needed a nap, but they didn't have time to rest.

They strolled in pretend casualness to a fleet of maintenance trucks, chose one at random, and jumped into the cab. Sol got it running, and they drove slowly to the Ratterran cruiser, next to an engine outtake.

Amaya got out of the truck and pretended to inspect the system with a scanner in her hand.

One of the Ratterran guards came up to her. "What are you doing?" he asked in Xiatat.

"This the ship called in for maintenance, right?" she said in English.

Sol had assured her the Ratterran wouldn't know her language, but an attempt to communicate calmly would make the Ratterran think the problem was on his end. It appeared Sol was right. The guard cocked his head quizzically and brought his com link up to his mouth.

Sol hit him on the back of the head, and the Ratterran went down with a thump. Leaving him there, Sol ambled over to the other guard outside the gangway into the ship. This guard must have been even less wary than the first because Sol had him down even faster. He dragged the second guard to the truck and dumped him inside before helping Amaya do the same to the first guard. Then they marched into the ship, with their scanners out, pretending to look for a problem.

When they noticed no one was within sight of the entrance, they continued to the cavernous holding area, past piles of crates and small ships tied down for future use.

Someone across the bay shouted at them.

Sol waved languidly, so Amaya stayed close to him.

As they approached the Ratterran who had shouted, Amaya stepped forward. "This is the ship that called for maintenance, right?" she repeated.

"What?" the Ratterran said back. "An Earther-Ratterran?"

"You speak English?"

"Who are you?" the Ratterran repeated and drew his weapon.

"Put it down, Ratterran scum." Sol drew his grenjen out and stepped in front of Amaya.

The Ratterran pointed his weapon at Sol. "Terr? How does one such as you come to be here with her?"

Sol shot the Ratterran in the leg and then hit him over the head. Then he pointed the grenjen at the man's head, with his finger on the trigger.

Amaya smacked Sol's wrist, forcing the grenjen

down. Anger bubbled inside her again, and her eyes grew hot. She knew she should look away, but instead, she stared Sol down. "What are you doing?! He hadn't fired on us!"

Sol's eyebrows raised, and he backed up. "You-your eyes."

"Stop trying to charm me, Sol! The only way we get out of here alive is by not killing people."

"No. I mean, yes. You're right. We can't kill all the Ratterrans. I won't." He held up his hands in front of his face, and then he knelt on the ground. "Please, Amaya. Your eyes are glowing like the sun."

"What is that supposed to mean?"

"How could you not know?" Sol trembled.

Amaya couldn't imagine what he meant about her eyes glowing like the sun. "I really don't know what you mean."

He peered up at her through his hands and got to his feet again. "It's gone, but…you had the power in your eyes." He pointed to the Ratterran on the ground between them. "And why did this Ratterran call you an Earther-Ratterran?"

"I don't know."

"He's still alive. I shot him in the leg. I didn't kill him," Sol said quietly. "Although it's a matter of time before he wakes up and tries to kill me."

Amaya sighed. "Maybe." She knelt over the Ratterran to bind the bleeding hole in his leg with a scarf he wore around his neck. As she worked, he opened his eyes.

"Rayatana? Is it you?"

"No, my name's Amaya."

"What did he call you?" Sol hovered over her shoulder.

"Rayatana." The Ratterran sighed and passed out.

Sol dug his fingers into her shoulder. "Look at me, Amaya. Are you the Rayatana?"

"What? The Rayatana? Are you crazy?" She shoved Sol's hand off her shoulder and glared at him.

His eyes widened, and he took a step back.

What is his problem? I'm not the Rayatana, some destined savior of The Great Galaxy. She had no idea what was going on, but asking Sol wasn't going to get her home any faster. She had to find his aunt and uncle so they could fly her home.

Waves of confusion, fear, and anger washed through her, but she ignored Sol and stormed into the ship, keeping her gaze down.

UNDER THE
CIRCUMSTANCES

Under the circumstances, Amaya knew she couldn't indulge in her anger. Plus, she didn't know where she was going. After charging ahead, she stopped at a junction in the ship's passageways. They'd come up one level from the cargo bay, and there were several ways to go from this point. They hadn't come across any other Ratterrans for Sol to injure, and her hot anger had ebbed.

Deciding to give Sol another chance, she asked, "Which way do we go?"

"We should split up. We can cover more ground." Sol didn't even look at her but took the left-hand hallway and started checking the rooms.

Amaya wasn't sure she trusted him, even with the tight pain in her chest alerting her to the strain on their Bond, but she went to the right anyway. The first room she came across was empty, and the second door was locked from the outside. She swiveled to look for Sol behind her, but he must've gone into one of the rooms.

She took a bobby pin out of her hair and inserted it into the lock, which looked like an Earth padlock. With a bit of a wiggle, she found the tumbler. Gently, she pushed and heard a satisfying click. After removing the lock off the door, she placed it quietly on the ground. Then she raised her weapon and opened the door.

A gorgeous-looking guy, with olive skin and dyed purple-black hair twisted in dreadlocks, lay on a cot. He opened his eyes and looked at her.

"Who are you?" His voice strummed a note in Amaya's heart. Her muscles relaxed, and she dropped her weapon to her side.

He was on his feet and across the room before she could get off a shot, but when he reached for her neck, she ducked and swept his legs out from under him. She brought her weapon up again. "You're not who I'm looking to rescue. Stay down or get shot."

He smiled lazily up at her from the floor. "I like a woman who takes control."

His voice could melt butter, but she didn't waver this time. "Do you know where Captain Prya and Galer are?"

"Auntie and Uncle found me? They're here?"

Suddenly, his looks went from charming to all-too-familiar. "Sol never mentioned a brother."

"Cousin Sol is here, too? It's a family reunion, except for you."

"How many family members do you have? I'm not sure I have time to find them all," she said dryly.

He laughed, and then his voice purred again. "Oh, just Auntie Prya, Uncle Geral, Sol's parents, my parents, my sister, and sweet, sexy me." He winked. "I like it when Sol brings me treats."

Amaya shot a hole in the floor by his leg.

He flinched. "Ooh, feisty."

The shot brought Sol running into the room. "What happened? Amaya, are you…?" His words trailed off when he looked at his cousin. "Chol." The name held a note of disbelief, mirrored with… disappointment? Amaya couldn't be sure she understood the nuances of Sol's tone, but he didn't sound ecstatic to find his cousin.

"Sol, you're with her? Amazing." Chol arched an eyebrow at Amaya. "What do you see in him?"

Amaya shook her head and lowered her weapon. "We're not together. I'm not available. And we're here on a mission to save your aunt and uncle, so cut the chit-chat. Let's find them, rescue their ship, and then I can get home."

"Girl has her priorities, Sol. Can you handle

that?" Chol rose languidly to his feet, stretching his arms to show off his impressive muscles.

"She's right," Sol growled. "Let's go the other way down the corridor. We don't have much time."

Amaya let the two of them check out the other end of the corridor, while she checked the rooms off this one. The last room had a tiny, retrofitted window with bars across it. She wondered why, until she looked inside. The whole cell was trashed. The cushion from the cot had been shredded, and no bedding or sheets were visible, other than as scraps.

A beautiful woman with pale skin and jaggedly cut luminescent-white hair sat slumped in one corner. She wore a sleeveless top and shorts. Scars crisscrossed her arms and legs.

Did the Ratterrans hurt her? Amaya didn't know who the good or the bad people were in The Thousand Years' War, but she didn't like seeing anyone suffer.

"Hey," Amaya called through the small window.

"Go away."

"Don't you want out?"

The woman opened her eyes, revealing bright purple irises with green pupils. She definitely wasn't human, Terr, or Ratterran. "Who are you? You're not one of them."

VISION

Suddenly, the woman's back arched, her eyes widened, and her green pupils grew until they eclipsed the violet around them. Her voice changed, growing deeper. "She is the Child of Three Worlds, the Rayatana, an ambassador, a hope for peace. She has three paths, three choices, three destinies. Love or peace or death." The woman shuddered, and she shook her head. When she gazed at Amaya again, she said, "Well, that sucks."

Amaya, who had been staring at her, started to laugh. It was a hysterical laugh, but the more it bubbled up, the more real it became. She leaned against the door and let it out. When she finally got herself under control, she picked the lock on the door and opened it. "Come on. We need to find Prya and Galer and get off this ship."

"You would free me?"

"Sure." Amaya couldn't imagine why the woman hesitated.

The woman nodded. "The first choice." She smiled, revealing sharp teeth. "I will protect you with my life, Child of Three Worlds."

"Amaya. Just call me Amaya." She really didn't want anyone else calling her the Rayatana or Child of Three Worlds, or anything else. She was an Earther. Not some prophesied peace-bringer.

"I am Tanwen Anadler tan Ddraig, Visionist. It is my full name. My secret name. Please tell others my name is Tanwen."

"I will."

She bowed from the waist with her hand to her forehead. "I am forever in your debt, Chain-breaker."

Amaya bowed in return. "Thank you, Tanwen."

"You honor me, Rayatana."

"No, I…am not sure if I am this Rayatana. I just want to get home and ask my mom some questions."

"Seeking knowledge is the way to find wisdom," Tanwen said solemnly. Then she gave Amaya a quirky smile. "At least that's what I have heard."

The way the woman bounced back and forth between solemnity and humor made Amaya smile. She waved her hand toward the hallway. "Let's go."

They exited the cell and turned to go down the

hallway back to the junction. Far down the hall, Sol and Chol left another cell, shouldering Galer between them. Galer was unable to hold weight on one of his legs. Behind them, Prya limped out of the cell. Amaya hurried toward them with Tanwen close behind. When they reached the others, Sol and Chol stopped.

Sol set his baleful gaze on Tanwen. "What are you doing here, traitor?"

Amaya bristled at his tone. Her anger returned, and heat pierced her eyes. The room brightened.

Sol covered his eyes. "Amaya, please?"

Chol's mouth dropped.

But Tanwen put a gentle hand on Amaya's arm and faced the others. "Sol, I have betrayed no one. Chol, you and I have broken trust with one another. The blame is not all mine. Because of you, we were both captured."

Chol grunted. For some reason, his disgruntlement made Amaya want to laugh. Because of that, her anger subsided, and the hallway returned to its normal brightness.

Tanwen continued to speak. "Amaya has rescued me. I am forever in her debt and will protect her against enemies and those who call themselves friends. She is the Child of Three Worlds, come to lead us to a new way."

Galer lifted his head to look at Amaya. "It is

true. There was something there before, but I did not see it clearly." He turned to Prya. "My love, our mission may have failed for the Terr Protectorate, but has succeeded for The Triple One."

Prya smiled wryly. "I disagree." She turned her attention to Sol. "Sol, you and your ability to run into trouble has saved us this time. You gave Amaya your Word and your Bond. She accepted both. It will not be easy, but you have created a way for peace." She placed her hand to her heart and bowed to Amaya. "Our family is honored by your Word, Amaya. My people will be honored by your Bond."

Chol raised an eyebrow at Amaya. "And you said you weren't together?"

"We aren't," Amaya growled. A sharp pain jabbed her in the chest, but she ignored it.

Wincing, Sol stepped forward. "She is…not a Terr. Aunt Prya, you can't hold us to our vow."

The pain in Amaya's chest increased, and she swallowed back a gasp.

"She didn't know what it meant," he continued. "I knew she didn't. It was—"

"The right vow at the right time. A choice made for a lifetime," Prya said. "You have saved our world."

"But not your way of life, Terr," Tanwen snapped.

Amaya shook her head. "We are not…it is

not…possible for us to be together, so you have nothing to worry about, Sol." But as soon as she said those words out loud, the pain ripped through her again. "Oh." She bent forward.

"You cannot break it." Tanwen put her hand on Amaya's shoulder. "I cannot protect you from choices you have already made. If it makes you feel any better, his denial hurts him, too." She pointed at Sol.

Amaya gazed at him.

Sol's face was tight, and he held one hand to his chest. "I don't want to break it. I want you to be free of it so you can return to your home on Earth without unwanted complications." He winced and dropped to one knee.

The pain echoed in her, and she gasped again. "We can't do this, Sol. It's hurting both of us too much." She reached out to him, and he took her hand. The pain immediately ebbed. "I accepted your Bond and gave you my Word. We will figure it out together."

He gave her a hopeful, puppy dog look.

"I am not promising anything other than close friendship," she said.

"But I can hope."

A zing of attraction raced through her, and she stepped back.

Chol whistled. "Well, this makes me glad for

the rescue, Cousin. At least you've brought some excitement back into our family. I can't wait to see how this unravels, especially with our favorite queen mother."

"Your mom is the queen?" She gaped at Sol.

"No, no. His mom is the queen." Sol pointed at Chol. "He's the Terr I was supposed to retrieve."

"Mommy dearest must have missed me to send you to my rescue." Chol rolled his eyes.

Sol glanced at Chol and then at Amaya. "This 'mommy dearest' means something I don't understand, doesn't it? More of the Earth pop slang."

"Yes," she said, and small bubble of happiness surged inside her at his recognition of Earth pop culture and slang. A second later, though, she squashed it down and frowned. "Let's get out of here, please. You can explain your large and weird family dynamics to me later."

AN INEVITABLE FIGHT

The exit was blocked by at least two dozen Ratterrans.

Sol let go of his uncle and stood next to her. When he spoke, his voice was strained. "Amaya, I understand you do not like killing, but I don't think we're going to get out of this without it."

She looked at him. "If you don't have a choice, if it is self-defense, I understand. But not until then."

"I will follow your lead." He nodded, but he held his grenjen in his hand.

"May I speak?" Tanwen offered.

Amaya took a step back.

Tanwen stepped between the two groups and held up her hands. "Ratterrans, still your weapons for the woman of three worlds, the Rayatana." She made a sweeping gesture to indicate Amaya.

Amaya's mouth dropped open, and then she closed it and lifted her chin, trying to look the part.

"The Rayatana is a myth!" One of the Ratterrans, the one wearing the most medals on his maroon space jacket, stated. He held his weapon in the air, but he kept the nose of it tilted down for safety. "And, if she is not, then she can prove herself to us."

Amaya's skin prickled in fear, but if she could prove herself, they could get out without bloodshed. *What did they expect me to do?*

"She has proven herself to me already, Captain," Tanwen explained. "And you know who and what I am."

He snorted. "You're a valuable prisoner, I admit. But just yesterday you were trying to kill yourself to escape. You'd do and say anything to get out of here."

Amaya stepped next to Tanwen. "What is it you would have me do to prove myself?"

"Fight me." The Ratterran stepped into the center of the cargo bay. "No weapons. Show me your skills. If you beat me, I will believe. If you even hold your own, I will consider it. If you lose, and lose badly, I will kill you and take your friends prisoner again."

"You will not kill her." Tanwen held out her hands. "One pulse from your friends' weapons and I will kill you all. You know I can do it. You managed to capture me because I was asleep."

"You were drunk." The man laughed. "Drunk on your dreams and more juice than you could handle."

"I'm not drunk now." Tanwen took a fighting stance. "Test me and see."

"No, no. We're testing her. Your Rayatana. Ray of Hope, Friend of the Stars, Xia's ass."

The man sauntered in the center of the cargo bay, flexing his muscles for his crew, mocking The Great Galaxy. He had thick arms, a wide chest, and tree trunk legs, but he also had a stiff shoulder and limped, favoring his right foot.

I might be able to take him.

"I will fight you." She lowered her grenjen to the ground, and kicked it over to Tanwen.

"Don't!" Sol put his hand on her arm. "Please, if anything happens to you…please, don't. The Bond between us is too strong. If one of us dies, both of us die."

Her throat tightened, and she swallowed nervously. That wasn't a complication she wanted for either of them.

She gazed up at him, this cute alien boy who had kidnapped her accidentally, taken her off her world, and showed her she was more than she even knew. He wasn't perfect, or necessarily good, but she didn't want to lose him or hurt him.

She shook her head at herself. *I'm an idiot.*

"Sol, if we're meant to be, then we will be. If not, I'm going to go out fighting for what I think is right in the way I think is right. We're just going to have to hope it doesn't kill either of us." She put her hand over his, gave it a squeeze, and then walked away from him.

In the center of the cargo bay, she blocked everyone else out and focused on the Ratterran captain. "May I know your name?"

His eyebrows rose. "You don't even know me? And you dare to challenge me?"

"I'm new to this. But I do know it's polite and customary to share at least first names in a match." She held her hand to her heart. "I am Amaya." She gave him a small head bow, not taking her eyes off him.

He stiffened at the gesture and placed his hand over his heart. "I am Captain Rayal." He also gave a small head bow, without looking away from her. When he broke formality, he loosened his shoulders and grinned. "And you can call me Captain Death."

Behind him, his crew cheered.

Amaya ignored them and launched into a feint toward his left cheek.

He side-stepped into her cross to his right shoulder, winced, and bounced back on his feet. Then his leg swept out. She jumped over it and countered by kicking his chest.

Even though he stepped back, she made contact. He was fast, though, and grabbed her foot, twisting it. She spun and kicked at his hands with her other foot, causing him to break away. She fell to the ground, into a roll, and popped back up as he bore down on her. Her jab and uppercut hit him in the gut, but he had her by the hair.

Tears sprang to her eyes as he yanked her hair, but she continued to punch him in the gut, in the chest, and finally, when he yanked upward, she landed an upper cut to his jaw.

He fell back, but he didn't let go of her hair, so she stumbled after him.

This time, he managed to hit her in the chest.

It hurt done-deep, but instead of falling back, she concentrated on forcing herself straight down, even with his hold on her hair. A searing pain in her scalp came as her hair ripped out, but it was worth it. She punched him in the knee. Then, with all of her momentum, she pushed up with her legs and punched him in the jaw again.

He let go of her and staggered backward. This time, she came after him.

When he tried to grab her, she spun around him and put him in a choke hold.

Pulling on her arm, he went down to his knees.

"Tap out," she told him. She didn't know if his alien culture would understand, but, apparently, he did, as he tapped her arm gently.

She let him go and sprang back, not touching any of the places where he'd hurt her. It was best to pretend those places didn't exist.

XIA'S OATH

"Xia's oath, you may be the Rayatana." Captain Rayal put one hand on his knee and rose slowly, gasping for breath.

Amaya watched him, taking shallow breaths. She didn't think any of her ribs were broken, but they might be bruised. The one hit he'd given to her chest had hurt as if she'd been kicked by a mule. She had to be careful about what she said next. While he was convinced, and Tanwen was convinced of her tri-world heritage, she wasn't sure.

If I accept it, what does it mean for me, now and later? And, what does accepting the debt of Tanwen really mean? I don't want another bond.

She wanted an explanation, but she couldn't get one in this tense moment.

Captain Rayal finally got to his feet. When he did, he put his fist to his heart and bowed low from the waist. "Command me, Rayatana Amaya. I am yours."

Amaya wanted to look to Tanwen for help, or to Sol for insight, but she put her palm to her heart and bowed her head. "I am honored, Captain Rayal. I am in need of a safe passage to Earth."

"Of course, I would be honored to give you a ride to your planet."

Tanwen stirred in the periphery of Amaya's vision. She glanced at the alien woman. It seemed, by her furrowed brow and slight shake of her head, she was warning Amaya.

Amaya had her own reservations about the Ratterran captain, and she couldn't give ground after a fight she'd barely won. "I would prefer to take the Terr ship to Earth with your ship as an escort."

Captain Rayal narrowed his eyes, but he nodded. "And after you return to Earth, what is to become of the Terr ship and the Terrs?"

She didn't like his line of questioning. It wasn't up to him as the loser of their match to steer this conversation or what happened to anyone. "It is no concern of yours."

"But I have ownership of the vessel, as a captured vessel of The Thousand Years' War."

"You have need of an S-29 class ship outfitted to blend in as an Earth movie theater? Do you plan to infiltrate Earth?"

He dropped his gaze to the ground. "We have scouts on Earth, as the Terrs do. It is not my area."

"So, you have no need of the ship. I do," Amaya said firmly. "If you are to be under my command, you will have to accept this."

"And what of my prisoners?"

"They are mine now." She wasn't going to explain herself to him. The more she thought about his questions and his pushiness, the angrier she became. Heat grew behind her eyes again. and she glared at Captain Rayal.

He squinted and stepped back. One of his hands fluttered up to his face, but then he dropped it to his side. "You did not show your power in our fight."

"I had no need." Actually, Amaya had no idea how to turn it off and on other than by getting angry, but she wasn't going to tell him that.

Trembling now, Captain Rayal got down on one knee and bowed his head. He put his fist to his heart again. "I will bow to your will in all things and ask only that you allow me to serve your cause."

Not wanting any more binding vows of loyalty, she stood there, staring at the captain, unsure of what to do. Finally, she thought of something. "Will you be in my…Honor Guard, Captain Rayal?"

He pressed his lips together in thought, glanced

at his crew, and then nodded once. "Yes, Rayatana."

She didn't want to push her luck, but she had to do something with him, something that might make sense to these military-minded people. "Appoint your second in command as the new captain of your ship and become a member of my Honor Guard. Tanwen will be your Commander."

Rayal's mouth opened, and then he bowed his head lower. "Yes, Rayatana."

He was still kneeling before her, and she stood in front of his crew with possibly cracked ribs and a handful of real allies. They had to move, or someone was going to figure out she was making this up as she went.

She waved her hand toward her group. "Rise and join my…people."

Rayal rose and joined the group by taking up a position next to Captain Prya, who stiffened as he approached. He glanced over his crew again. "Lieutenant Jaynus, I appoint you as Captain. You will have to make yourTrial after we return the Rayatana to Earth."

"What does that mean, Rayal?" Amaya wanted to ensure she wasn't getting stabbed in the back through some code language.

"To gain rank, we fight our way to the top. Only the strongest may lead."

"I am their leader, then?"

The Ratterran crew grumbled, but they subsided when a huge man with long blonde dreadlocks stepped forward and saluted Rayal, then pivoted to salute Amaya.

"Rayatana, our crew is yours, by right of rank and Trial."

Amaya saluted in return.

Right then, a young girl with dark skin and close-cropped curls stepped away from the Ratterran crew. "Father?"

Rayal held out his arms, and the girl ran into them. "Bay, I…" He glanced at Amaya. "May I bring my daughter with me, Rayatana?"

"Yes, of course." She couldn't believe he would have left his daughter.

Bay glared at Amaya from her father's arms.

So be it. Amaya couldn't change the girl's mood. She needed to get medical help, get home, and get answers.

Taking shallow gasps of air, she tried not to show how weary she felt. "We must be on our way."

Rayal held up his hand. "Are you sure there is nothing more you need to complete your mission?"

"At this time—" She glanced at the others, then at Tanwen, who had one of her eyebrows cocked.

"At this time, I need more information. Do you have a memory-cube I may take on Ratterran history and culture?"

Rayal nodded. "Yes. When I get on board their ship, I will program a cube with our history and culture, especially our dealings with the Terrs." He glanced at Sol and then back at Amaya. "They are not as honest as they claim to be, Rayatana."

"I think there is always more than one side to a story," she said as diplomatically as she could. She hadn't liked the taste of the brutal power structure of the Ratterrans, but she was still floundering to understand her role and couldn't afford to make them angry.

Rayal gave her a short salute and stepped back. Then he turned to the other Ratterrans. "Let them pass!"

They parted, crowding to either side of the gangway exiting the cargo bay.

With her head held high, Amaya walked past the Ratterrans, with Tanwen to her right side, Sol and Chol half-carrying Galer to her left, and the two Ratterrans on the outside of Captain Prya. It took all her will power to walk forward evenly, as every step jarred her ribs. She hoped she could keep up the façade, because she couldn't appear weak and they needed off this ship.

YOU KNOW

"You know they don't always keep their Word," Sol whispered to Amaya as she entered his aunt and uncle's spaceship through the movie theater lobby.

Amaya didn't look at him. From what she'd gained from the Terr memory-cube, their hatred of the Ratterrans ran deep and raw, from hundreds of years of assassination attempts, conflicts, and contempt. But underneath, their cultures were branched from the same roots.

"Amaya," Sol whispered again.

"I heard you, Sol." She took his hand in hers. "I know you mean well. I know you are indebted to me, and our words, however foolish, will hold us to our Bond, which is deeper than I realized. But the same Bond does not force us to trust one another. We're going to have to work on that." She glanced at Rayal and Bay, who appeared to be hanging on to their conversation.

She sighed. "Captain Prya, how soon until we can fly to Earth?"

"As soon as we take flight. The Ratterrans made repairs to our lifters." Prya held her injured side, but she glanced at Galer. "Our consoles can keep us going with photo-medicine until we get there."

Prya and Chol helped Galer to his seat in the command center. He immediately used the photo-medicine hooked into his console. "These…will…keep me steady until we get where we need to go, with our escort." He glared at Rayal.

"We are here to make sure the Rayatana stays safe." Rayal took up a position inside the box office command center and strapped into a jump seat that folded down from the wall. He nodded to his daughter. "Take the Med-bay."

She nodded and walked out, which freed up some of the space inside.

Chol went for the seat previously occupied by Amaya.

"No, Chol." Prya stopped him. "Amaya will sit there, Tanwen will sit in the jump seat behind her, Sol will have his usual seat, and you will take a seat in the Med-bay, the safest place outside of this booth."

"Don't speak to Bay," Rayal snapped.

"Afraid she'll fall to my charm?" Chol purred in his sexiest voice.

Amaya gritted her teeth. Chol's voice might affect her enough to annoy her, but to think he might use it on someone who would be swayed by it was not something she would tolerate. "Chol, you will not charm her while I'm on this ship."

"Thank you, Rayatana." Rayal nodded to her.

"Right," Chol said. "Until we meet again, Rayatana." Sarcasm dripped over her title. But, before she could say anything, he grabbed her hand and pressed a kiss to it.

She yanked her hand away, but as she did, he slipped a flat rectangle into her fingers. She didn't know why he would pass her something, but she cupped it in her hand. "You're such a creep."

Chol waggled his eyebrows. "Oh, you say that now." He sauntered out of the room.

Next to her, Sol sighed. "I'm sorry, Amaya."

His apology for his cousin's behavior softened her feelings toward him even more. "You can't control him, Sol."

"I know. I can only keep my Word." He gazed at her.

Sincerity shone in his eyes. The zing of attraction and warmth from the Zoe Bond startled her, and she looked away.

What am I going to do? I'm only seventeen.

Even if Sol hadn't been an alien, even if she was the Rayatana, even if the situation wasn't complicated, she wouldn't throw herself into a serious relationship, especially not a romance with a "Bond" that might as well scream old-fashioned betrothal.

"To Earth, Rayatana?" Prya asked, breaking into her thoughts.

"Yes, let's go home." Going home wouldn't solve everything. She wasn't even sure it would solve anything, but she longed for home, for her mom, and for the answers to her questions. If her mom wouldn't answer her, maybe her dad could. *His work for the Space Defense Force had to be good for something other than keeping him away from home.*

As the others busied themselves at their consoles, she glanced down at what Chol had pressed into her hand. It was a chip with a constellation marking on it, and the constellation made five circles, linked together. One of the stars was inked in green. She glanced around, not sure if she should show it to anyone, and slipped it into a pocket on her coveralls.

ZERO INERTIA GRAVITY
DRIVE AKA ZIG

"Zero Inertia Gravity Drive, countdown," Galer said, "10, 9, 8, 7, 6, 5, 4, 3, 2, 1, ZIG."

This time, Amaya tapped the photo-medicine button twice, preparing herself for the gut-wrenching jump through space and hoping it would ease her pain. Her ribs still ached, but she kept her eyes mostly open to see a blinding blur of stars in the black. When they slowed, Earth hung like a blue jewel in the dark atmosphere. The sun was behind them. The moon, in her orbit, looked calm. Amaya breathed a sigh of relief.

Home. I'm home again. Or at least in orbit.

"Where should we land our ship?" Prya asked.

Amaya pressed her lips together, trying to think. She glanced at Sol, to Rayal, to Tanwen, to Galer, and then back to Prya, sitting straight in her captain's chair console. "My grandparents' old farm is out of town, sheltered from view by foothills on three sides. I know that won't help with getting past the Space Defense Force, but there aren't any neighbors for miles."

Prya nodded curtly. "We'll take care of the detection issues." She tilted her head to Sol. "Cloaking online?"

"Yes, Captain."

"I don't suppose you know coordinates, like longitude and latitude?" she asked Amaya.

"Um." Amaya knew them. She used to think her mom was weirdly obsessed with knowing longitude and latitude for wherever they lived, but now…things from her childhood were falling into place. "47.1734° N, 121.9733° W."

Sol gazed at her. "How do you know them so well? Coordinates are not covered in Earther schools."

"My parents." She shrugged. "My dad thought it was useful knowledge, and my mom had a thing about knowing our coordinates, as well as our street address. I didn't understand it…until now." Everything she'd thought she'd known was like the crust on a mystery meat pie. Her mom was obviously alien. That must have been what her dad had meant about immigration issues. He hadn't been talking about the United States immigration laws. "My mom taught me a lot, but she kept a lot hidden."

"She sounds like a wise woman," Tanwen said.

Rayal laughed. "A wise Ratterran spy knows how to get found and how to stay hidden."

"Terr spies know this, as well," Galer said. He glanced at Amaya. "Do you know if your mother is Terr or Ratterran?"

Amaya shook her head. "No." She put her hand to her necklace, but she didn't show it to them.

"It does not matter," Prya said. "Lock in the coordinates, Galer. Take us down."

"What of the Ratterran ships?" Rayal demanded.

His words were lost as the ship dipped nose-first and flew swiftly toward the surface of Earth. The atmospheric entry created a cacophony of noise. Once they reached visual distance of the small farmstead, Galer rotated the ship and backed it down onto the land near Amaya's home, on the other side of a copse of trees.

"The Ratterran ships were detected on our entry." Sol tapped the buttons on his console. "And their detection has led the US Space Defense Force to recognize our entry as well. We have a limited time frame until they, or the military, arrive."

"If you had contacted Captain Jaynus." Rayal pointed his finger at Prya.

"Not now. I need to get my mom." Amaya

tapped the photo-medicine button again before unstrapping herself and walking out of the command console, not waiting for anyone to follow. The photo-medicine was only dulling the pain, but she had to get to her mom quickly.

As she exited the ship, her mom came out of the house, wearing a military uniform and carrying a huge military duffel bag.

"Mom!"

"Amaya!" Her mom threw her arms around her and hugged her close.

Amaya winced from the pain in her ribs. "Mom. I'm hurt."

Her mom drew back and gazed into her eyes. "We have to leave. I don't have time to explain everything, but your dad will do what he can to scramble the Space Defense Force's tracking systems. He'll buy us time to leave."

"What?" The tears Amaya had been holding back under her bravado welled up in her eyes.

"I'm coming with you. You're too important to lose to Earth's squabbling politics." She started toward the ship.

Amaya stood still, staring at her mom's back. *Has she known I'm the Rayatana? A prophesied peace-bringer or leader?* All the training, all the private schools, the way her mom had chosen her friends, everything clicked into place. And the anger she'd always struggled to contain erupted with intense heat from her eyes.

Rays of light slammed into her mom's back, knocking her mom to the ground.

Amaya shut her eyes. *No, no, no. I don't want to hurt her. Not like this. No.* The heat felt like a thousand suns pushing against her eyelids.

The sound of running footsteps came toward her. Long fingers touched her arm, and Sol's touch calmed her.

He spoke quietly. "Breathe, like you did on the climb down from the space ship. One breath at a time. You can control this."

She took in a shaky breath, but it came out on a sob. "My mom?"

"Tanwen is seeing to her."

"Will she be okay?"

"You stopped the burst mid-stream. She will live."

"She never wanted me to look at anyone in anger."

Sol snorted. "Obviously, you need training."

"Can *you* train me?"

He squeezed her to his chest. "Uncle Galer can. And I can help with the basics. I had to learn them when I was a child. My gift is mainly my voice, but I do have some of the light. Both are weak for a Terr of the royal line. They are not easy gifts to bear."

"I can imagine."

He laughed. "Most people would want your gift."

"I don't."

"You can open your eyes. I trust you."

She pressed herself against his chest for another moment. Then she looked down and to the side before opening her eyes slowly. She didn't feel the heat. No glowing rays or brightness lit up the grass. Gradually, she shifted her gaze to where Rayal cradled her mom in his arms, while Tanwen pressed a glowing hand to her back.

Her awe of the older woman increased. *What is she?*

"We need to get her to Med-bay. I can't do more than stabilize her here," Tanwen said.

"Thank you," Amaya said.

Tanwen and Rayal carried her mom toward the theater-spaceship, sitting haphazardly in the old cow pasture.

Amaya looked up to find Sol gazing down at her. Gold flecks shimmered in his eyes. He leaned down until his lips nearly touched hers, but then he paused.

Amaya closed the distance and kissed him. Another warm jolt of attraction raced through her, and she struggled to keep the kiss brief, just a soft press of her lips against his. After a moment, she ducked her head and pulled away. "We need to go."

"Amaya." His voice was husky.

Flashing lights of police vehicles coming up the long driveway forced her attention back to their danger.

"Run!" She grabbed his hand and tried to run for the theater-spaceship, but the pain in her ribs stopped her stride.

"I can carry you." Sol scooped her up before she could respond.

The jolt of his steps still hurt as he ran, but it was better than trying to run.

Inside, Sol shouted across the lobby to the others. "I need to get her to Med-bay!"

"No! I need to be in the command center." She struggled against him until he let her slide out of his embrace. "I need to know what's going on when we leave. And I can take more of the photo-medicine. I didn't realize it would wear off so soon."

"The gift overwhelms any photo-medicine you take, especially anything that would dull your senses." He walked her back to the command center and helped her into her seat before taking his own.

Once she had taken more of the photo-medicine for pain, she focused on relaxing her muscles and gazed out the viewport at her home. Blackberries and tall grass had overrun much of her grandparent's farm. The old workshop and barn were gray with age. The two-story yellow house that always smelled like jam or pickles looked tiny and forlorn. Even if it hadn't been her home for long, it represented everything she had to leave behind. Home would have to become where her heart resided, where she could be free and safe, where she had a purpose.

She nodded to Prya. "Let's go."

Galer started the ship's engines.

Prya gave the command.

And they lifted off, flying to the stars.

A MISSED CONVERSATION

Once they reached orbit, Amaya stared out the viewports at the blueness of Earth.

Two ships streaked to meet them, sleek and full of power. The Ratterran ships were beautiful. All the same, Amaya was glad to be in the movie-theater spaceship.

Another ship, bulkier and bristling with outer weapons exited Earth's atmosphere and trundled toward them.

"We've got an incoming message from the U.S. Space Defense Force," Galer said.

"Amaya?" Captain Prya swiveled her chair to face her. "I think I need to take this."

Amaya nodded.

Prya punched a button on her console. "U.S. Space Defense Force, this is Captain Prya of the Terr Protectorate."

"Alien vessels, this is Commander Gray Benson of Earth Champion 2DZ, requesting that you return to Earth at once."

"Dad?" Amaya couldn't believe she was hearing his voice.

"That's really your dad?" Sol asked.

Amaya nodded, swallowing back the tightness in her throat.

Prya pointed at Amaya's armrest. "You need to hit the communication button. It's the green one."

She clicked the transmission button. But then she clicked it off and glanced at Tanwen. "Who does the Rayatana lead? What are we called now?"

Tanwen's lips quirked, and then she frowned. "It is not good to admit such lack of knowledge in the presence of possible enemies."

"No one here is her enemy," Captain Prya stated sternly.

"What do you call the Rayatana movement?" Amaya asked.

"The Way of the Togetherness of All Peoples." Tanwen intoned the words as if they were part of a religious ritual.

"Okay, that's a bit long, and I need my dad to understand it, so I have another idea." She turned away from Tanwen to stare at the ship hovering on her viewscreen and clicked the transmission button. "Dad, it's me, Amaya. I've been named Rayatana of The Great Galaxy Alliance."

"Amaya? Baby, what are you doing there? Your mother said —"

A crackling noise cut them off.

What had happened? Amaya hit the communications button again, but they kept getting static.

Another voice cut in over her dad's. "Admiral Anderson speaking on behalf of Earth Champion 46DZ, Commander Gray Benson has been relieved of command. We cannot respond to an alien threat with a fatherly embrace. I will not go easy on you or your new friends, Amaya."

Out of all the people her dad worked with, it would have to be Anderson. She disliked him as much as he despised her.

"Admiral, please put my dad back on the comm," she said, trying to force her voice to remain calm. She hadn't parted on best terms with her dad after the divorce, but he was her dad, and she loved him. She swallowed back a sob. "I would like to say goodbye."

"Exactly what does that mean, Miss Benson?" Admiral Anderson's voice was terse but condescending.

"My alliance and I are leaving the Solar System. I would like to say goodbye to my dad."

"What were you doing on Earth?"

Before Amaya could respond, Prya made a chopping motion with her hand.

Amaya clicked off the transmission button. Tears came to her eyes and her throat ached, but she knew this was goodbye.

Gelar pointed at his screen. "They've launched another ship from their orbiting station. We need to leave before we get involved in a battle with a neutral zone planet."

On screen, a glowing blip separated from the orbiting Space Defense Station and started toward them.

"I'm sorry, Amaya, but I have to agree with Gelar on this," Prya said.

Amaya wiped away the tears on her cheeks with the back of her hand. "I understand."

Sol reached across the divide between their seats, but she shook her head at him.

"Destination coordinates?" Captain Prya asked.

Amaya reached into her pocket and pulled out the chip Chol gave her. "We go here." She showed the chip to Captain Prya, who's jaw tensed.

"How did you get that?"

"Chol gave it to me."

"Of course, he did." Captain Prya cleared her throat. "That's Ganyth System in Arm 5 of The Great Galaxy. It is under Terr control, guarded by our largest armada of ships. It is the heart of the Thousand Years' War."

A rush of information from the memory-cube filled Amaya's thoughts, but she resisted it with willful determination. The information was foreign to her but embedded in her mind. She wondered for a moment if she would ever be able to get rid of it. It was useful, no doubt about that, but it didn't contain everything she needed to know, like a warped encyclopedia filled with only half the information from the Terr-Ratterran cultures. She wanted the information she could gain from the Ratterran memory-cube, but she didn't want to overwhelm her brain.

How can I gain the information without harming myself?

"Amaya?" Tanwen laid a hand on her shoulder.

Amaya blinked and shook her head. "I was trying to separate the memory-cube information from my own thoughts. I guess I got lost for a moment."

Tanwen squeezed her shoulder. "It has been five Terr minutes. Long enough that we began to grow concerned, especially since you did not respond to the last question Captain Prya asked of you."

"You resisted the memory-cube?" Sol's eyebrows raised. "Why?"

"It has only half the information I need, maybe not even that."

He dropped his gaze. "I'm sorry, Amaya. I thought it would help you."

"It is a sign of her culture and her role," Tanwen stated solemnly. "She questions our way and makes her own path."

A loud ping sounded from Sol's console. He ran his fingers over the surface. "We have incoming weapon fire from the Earth ship."

Slow-moving compared to laser fire, Amaya guessed they were nukes. Her stomach tightened in terror.

"Avoidance maneuvers. Now." Gelar gave them a tiny warning before slamming the ship to the right.

Tanwen was out of her seat belts, but she crouched by Amaya's chair. Her hands morphed, elongating into claws, which she dug into the movie theater carpet and the metal underneath it.

Amaya's mouth dropped open. "Tanwen?"

The ship banked, dipped, and rolled. Tanwen stayed still; her muscles straining slightly with the pressures.

Amaya continued to stare at the woman she'd named leader of her Honor Guard. There was so much she didn't know, and she had to make decisions based on alien ideas and alien suggestions. *Was Admiral Anderson right to fire upon their ship?*

Galer chuckled as the weapon fire slid past them and their two Ratterran allied ships. "Earth has made great progress, but they aren't in our league."

Amaya wasn't sure that was reassuring. Even if she wasn't completely human, Earth was still her home.

"Regardless, we need a destination, and I would like to make a suggestion to the Rayatana." Captain Prya steeled her fingers. "If I may?"

"Of course." Amaya wished she could give over all of her responsibilities to Prya, but she couldn't because of the biases between Ratterrans and Terrs. Suggestions could help, though.

"I think we should return to the neutral planet, where you rescued us from our newfound Ratterran allies. It is not a place anyone would expect us to go. From there, we can make plans for Ganyth. And I can, or we can, find out why Chol gave you that chip."

Amaya didn't like the idea of going backward, but Prya had made good points. She glanced at Tanwen, who had resumed her humanoid form and taken her seat. "What do you suggest?"

Tanwen dipped her head to Prya. "Ganyth is not a place we should go without preparation. I do not trust the intentions of Chol in giving you the chip, and we need a place to recover from our wounds." Tanwen put her hand to her heart. "The honorable Captain is right to choose Cheleth, planet of the Raya."

Captain Prya's eyes widened. "That planet is of the Order? But it isn't on our charts."

"The Order wanted it to remain hidden until the Rayatana came." Tanwen smiled widely, revealing pointed incisors.

Amaya held up her hands. "I need to know all of this. I know I do, but my ribs are at least bruised, Galer is injured, my mom is…hurt, and we all need to rest." She leaned back and tried to use her hands to take off some of the weight from her injuries. The pressure made her gasp, despite the photo-medicine. "Please set a course for Cheleth."

"Galer, prepare us for ZIG. Destination: Cheleth." Captain Prya nodded to Amaya. "Send a message to Captain Jaynus of the Ratterran ships."

Amaya opened up the transmission button. Sol showed her how to direct it to the Ratterran ships, and she passed on the information.

Captain Jayrus made a sputtering sound. "B-but we were just there."

"Set a course," Amaya ordered him. Then she clicked off the transmission button, put her hands together, and closed her eyes. She tried to pray, but she didn't know what words to use. She was bossing aliens around and plotting a course to an alien solar system.

I have to be strong.

After praying for strength, she opened her eyes to see Tanwen and Sol staring at her.

Tanwen nodded and closed her eyes. "It begins."

Amaya glanced over at Sol. She flicked her gaze to Tanwen and back to him.

He smiled and held out his hand. This time, she entwined her fingers with his, noticing again the way they tapered more than hers, but also their warmth and strength. More than ever, she needed the lifeline he offered.

Galer began the countdown to ZIG.

As the ship punched into ZIG and the stars became streaks of brightness around them, Amaya kept her eyes wide open.

BRIEF GLOSSARY OF TERMS

Note: Some terms have more than one definition

Tuigseach: any intelligent life form or people group, and an important term for understanding the glossary

Cheleth: a neutral zone planet

Ddraigons: tuigseach who resemble Earth's idea of dragons

Ddraigon Kins: tuigseach formed by Ddraigon and another species

Awak: a stimulating drink, normally served warm, much like coffee or tea

Earthborn: any tuigseach born on Earth

Dryadarians: tuigseach who have plant and humanoid forms

Gifts/Powers: abilities which enable a tuigseach to do things against the laws of Xia

Granchan: a hearty stew made with fruits and vegetables, originated on Verde

Grenjen: a photo weapon

Glowers: tuigseach who love being mysterious

Memory-cube: a device which downloads information into the minds of most tuigseach

Nardels: a native animal of Cheleth, hunted to near-extinction

Photo-medicine: medicine based on light waves and particles

Order of Raya: those who have dedicated their lives to the Rayatana

Rayatana: Child of Three Worlds prophesied to end The Thousand Years' War; or, Friend of the Stars

Ratterrans: tuigseach who broke from the Terrs

Ratterran Alliance: an alliance of nine planets formed by the Ratterran Elite

Space Defense Force: an Earth-based space defense system

Terrs: tuigseach residing on the planet Terran in the Faran Galaxy

Terr Protectorate: nine planets and a solar system under the protection of the Terr Empire

The Great Galaxy: Earthborn call it The Milky Way Galaxy

The Thousand Years' War: an ongoing conflict between Terrs and Ratterrans

The Triple One: sometimes called the Three-in-One God of the Universe

Verde: the home planet of the Dryadarian

Xiatat: a universal language and money system for trade between tuigseach

Xia: another name for The Great Galaxy; or, a being worshiped by many

THANK YOU FOR READING THIS NOVELLA!

I wrote it during quarantine in April 2020, when I really needed to escape into a different world. I leaned into tropes, thought of it originally as an action-adventure "popcorn book" the way I often refer to certain, enjoyable but lighthearted movies as "popcorn movies." I enjoyed writing it and I hope you enjoyed reading it!

Originally, it wasn't my intent to create a series, but along the writing path, the characters became more and more intriguing, and The Great Galaxy threw the doors wide open to my imagination. As this book goes to print, I have finished the first, extremely rough draft of *Labyrinthine: Rayatana Series, Book 2.* Before I can share even a sneak peek, this second novella really needs some editing help from my trusty editor Chrys Fey, feedback from my Beta readers, and formatting from my wonderful formatting expert Carrie Butler.

If you are interested in being the first to know when the next novella is prepared to launch into the world, please consider following me on social media, or signing up for my very new newsletter. You can find me on Twitter, Instagram, and at my blog Tyrean's Writing Spot (named after Winnie-the-Pooh's Thoughtful Spot" or at my new website: Tyrean's Tales.

Again, thank you for going with me on this
exciting journey of writing imagination into space!

ACKNOWLEDGEMENTS

This book would not be possible without the encouragement and help I received from several amazing people.

First, I need to thank my editor and top cheerleader, Chrys Fey. Chrys Fey's specific comments and changes suggested on the manuscript helped me ground my writing in good mechanics and good pacing. In addition to the professional, critical feedback she gave, she sprinkled in encouraging words to keep me going in the right direction. Plus, she's an editor who goes above and beyond in the way she encourages authors. She knew I was struggling with some revisions, and she sent me a playlist she'd been listening to while editing. It brightened my day and really helped me tackle that tough part of the writing process. Many, many thanks to Chrys!

Second, I need to thank my excellent book cover artist and interior formatting expert, Carrie Butler. While it isn't anywhere in her job description, she also encouraged me to finish and helped me envision my book as a sold, finished entity. Thank you, Carrie!

Next, I need to thank the bloggers, Facebook friends, Wattpad readers, and commenters who read the first, extremely short novelette draft of *Liftoff*, when it was called *Crash*, during the April 2020 A to Z Challenge. Patricia Lynne was my top encourager throughout the month with comments on nearly every post. Thanks to everyone's comments and encouragement, I finished the first, hole-ridden draft and gained insights into how I might make it more complete.

Also, I need to thank my Thursday Write-In Critique Group. These five writers and I have helped each other refine our drafts and complete our projects. Thank you, Elizabeth, Kathy, Cindy, Julia, and Jana. I finally finished one of the four projects I made you read!

In addition to all of these professionals, writers, and commenters, I need to thank my parents for their all-around reading of various drafts. Plus, I need to thank my youngest daughter for her insights on voice, dialogue, realism for YA readers, character arcs, and pacing.

Last, but definitely not least, I need to thank my husband John who listens to me rant about my writing, asks questions about my my ideas, and gives me helpful ideas for rough versions of my book read out loud in the car. He gave me critical and supportive feedback when I read the "almost" final draft out loud to him on a long car drive across the state. Thank you, John, for discussing inertial dampeners and warp/space travel technology with me. For you, I added a reference to your favorite science fiction universe of all time. Did you see it?

www.ingramcontent.com/pod-product-compliance
Lightning Source LLC
Chambersburg PA
CBHW021703110726
47902CB00007B/2041